Cravings
A (Mostly) Fictional Memoir

by

Juliet James

Crooked Circle Press™

Bailey, CO / 2025

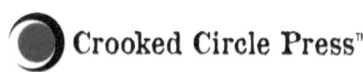 **Crooked Circle Press**™

Book Cover by Monika de los Rios.

Edited by Thomas James.

ISBN: 979-8-9888904-2-3

Library of Congress Control Number: 2025934413

First Edition

For Jean, who believed in me when I couldn't

and

For Thomas, I am so glad I needed orange juice. ;)

Table of Contents

Prologue

When I was writing this journal 25 years ago, I never imagined publishing it one day. In fact, I would've been horrified by the very thought! However, about a year ago, I stumbled upon a box of my old diaries, and this one stood out to me. It was fascinating to read the words of my younger self at such a pivotal moment in my personal history. I shared it with a friend, and they suggested that I publish it. I laughed, but they were very serious.

I dismissed the idea as absurd. Who would want to read my old journals? Yet, the idea wouldn't leave me alone, and a month later, I thought, well, it's worth a try, right?

I didn't imagine it would go anywhere, and for a while, it didn't. Then I got a call from Crooked Press Circle, an indie publisher in Colorado who loved my writing. Fast forward a bit, and well, here we are.

My greatest wish is for someone like me to read this and to feel less alone, and by someone like me, I mean someone the world seems to have disregarded for any reason. I hope that if you fit that description, when you've finished reading, you feel more hopeful.

Please note that I've changed some names and descriptions to protect the innocent (and not so innocent, in some cases).

XOXO,
Tessa Elizabeth Alexander

December, 1998

December 28, 1998

Dear Book,

I haven't written in a diary in like ten years, not since high school when my nosy Aunt Jane found my diaries, and I had to lie and tell her the stories I'd confessed about being fingered by my boyfriend Tim were not really my stories at all. I told Jane that they were my best friend Vanessa's diaries and her experiences. Jane had talked to her friend Johan, who is a psychiatric nurse, and he told her I was likely writing fantasies to make me feel better about myself. Oh, yeah. Because no one would want to finger me, right? Wrong. Tim did, and more than once. Pfft.

Anyway, I feel stupid writing Dear Diary. So I guess you're Dear Book. Which, when I stop and think about it, isn't really any less stupid, but at least it feels less childish somehow.

You were a Christmas gift from my dad's sister, Josephine, and her new girlfriend, Rainbow (yes, that is her real name). I love Aunt Jo, but she's not terribly great

3

with gift giving, so I'm fairly sure Rainbow influenced her heavily this year. I got you and a $50 gift card to Barnes & Noble, which I am pretty sure is the happiest place in the universe.

I should introduce myself. I mean, not that you are a sentient being or anything, but well, whatever. Writing helps me process. And yeah, I need to process who I am. Who doesn't, really?

I'm Tessa. I love little kids and made a career out of it, albeit one that pays shit money. I currently work with toddlers at a daycare center. It's one of the few things in my life I know I am damn good at. I've been doing it for several years now, and the kids and their parents all love me (with the rare exception because there is always one parent in every class who cannot be pleased, no matter what you do).

Anyway, it's that time of year. Post Christmas, pre New Years. So, naturally I'm feeling introspective and annoyed. I hate that whole *hey, it's the end of year, let's mentally rehash all the shit I didn't accomplish this year that I wanted to or meant to or thought I should* kind of stuff. I hate New Year's. I hate January. The pretty lights and sparkling decor of Christmas are boxed away, leaving January a bleak, blank slate of cold, grey weather and short days. People are full of (generally fake) positive energy about the New Year and all of the **things** they're going to accomplish! I hate resolutions. It's not like I've ever kept a single one. Fuck, I'm lucky if I make it out of January with one. In fact, I don't think I ever have. Once, when I was not quite 16, I had a list 16 resolutions (one for every year of my life). What the fuck was I thinking? Oh, wait. I wasn't. Of course, none of them was accomplished, and I probably forgot about most of them by the second week of January.

Still, I find myself thinking that if I make a list of **objectives** for 1999 *today* (instead of on New Year's Eve or New Year's Day), that means I haven't made "New Year's

4

Resolutions." If I'm calling them something like "goals" or "objectives," is that different? Or is it just semantics? It's probably semantics, but it feels less loaded. Also less bandwagon-y. I pride myself on being uniquely me, so doing something just because everyone else is... well... it annoys me. I never understood the popular kids in school for that reason. Who wants to sacrifice what they want to do or wear in order to please the Queen (or King) of the school? And then all the pressure to make sure you don't fall from "grace." No thanks. I'll stick with being happily unpopular.

And I guess that's part of why I hate resolutions so much. It's just what it seems like virtually everyone does this time of year. Yet, the thing is, I'm tired of being afraid to live my life.

Did I mention that I'm fat? I probably should've (this is undoubtedly why Jane and Johan couldn't possibly imagine I'd have a boyfriend). Not fat like my friends who are 5'5" and 150 lbs telling me how fat they are (ugh, sometimes I hate them even when I love them). No, I am *actually* fat. I'm probably like 400 lbs or something, and I am going to rejoin Fat Fighters in January because they'll be running their specials. But it's not a resolution. I swear. I'm just doing it then because it will be free to join. And I guess I decided that in 1999 I'm either going to *do something* about my weight or accept being fat **forever**. That part feels a bit resolution-y, but I'm going to attempt to ignore that by saying it's *just a goal*.

I also really need to learn to drive already. I mean, it's not like it's easy getting around without a car. I rely on Vanessa (my best friend since I was 4) or my mom for rides to work, which is kinda humiliating, to be honest. I don't know how I'd afford a car on my salary, but I could maybe at least borrow my mom's. Of course, it's a stick, which adds an entire layer of difficulty to the equation. Or so I hear. I've never driven any car, so what the fuck do I know? Not to mention I am not convinced my mother can teach me to drive without one of us killing the other.

I need to get back to dating, too. Not to "find the one" or anything. I've sort of given up on that dream. But I'm young, and I want to have fun, at least. I lived in Pennsylvania with my dad and his idiot wife (Carly) for four years, and while there I started using this telephone dating service. It's like the phone equivalent of newspaper personal ads; in fact it's oh-so-cleverly called Voice Personals. I met a lot of guys and had a lot of bad first dates, a few good ones, and virtually no second ones. Apparently guys are more than happy to make out with a fat chick, but they don't want to date her. Assholes.

I moved back to New Jersey, where I was born and grew up, in May and discovered there was a NJ version of Voice Personals (which is free for women seeking men - one of the rare perks of having a fucking uterus in my experience). I've called, and while I've talked to a lot of guys, I've had very few dates with any of them.

I have been holding back for some reason. Maybe I'm just tired of not getting second dates even when I felt like the first went really well.

There's a guy named Nick I've been talking to for like five months now, and he's been dying to meet me, but I don't know... I feel like he just wants to hook up with me because I have big boobs, and he's into that. Then again, I haven't really done much hooking up of late (as in none since moving back here), so maybe I should stop overthinking it and just meet him. What's the worst that could happen? I hate him and leave early?

I just want 1999 to be different. I want to look back someday and say *"That's the year. That's the year I changed my life forever."*

There's this guy who delivers for Domino's. He's pretty cute, and I've had a crush on him since I moved back here almost eight months ago. Maybe I'll slip him my number next time I order. I have no idea what his name even is, but hey - worst that happens is he never calls, right?

In fact, I'm going to do that tonight. I need food, anyway. I'm babysitting Olivia (my 7-year-old baby sister) tonight while our mother works. I know Livvy will be thrilled to have pizza.

Yeah, this feels like a good plan.

Okay, I grabbed a piece of stationery that has my name on it in a hot pink heart. I don't even know where I got this from, since I don't particularly like pink. Or hearts. Or anything overly cutesy. I've never even used it before, but I figured maybe it would be more flirtatious than plain paper. So, there it is... my name in a hot pink heart, and my number written below in purple ink. Nothing else. Maybe he'll be intrigued. Maybe *mysterious* can work for me.

Or maybe he's going to laugh his ass off at it.

But hey, at least I'll know I've done it, right?

Now, I think I'll call Nick to set up a date. Maybe.

XOXO,

Tessa

December 29, 1998

Well, I did it. I slipped *Pizza Guy* my number! I basically wrapped it inside the tip (which of course was generous). I can't believe I did it. I doubt he'll call. I feel half proud of myself for doing something so brazen and half stupid for thinking a cute guy would call me.

But hey, I said I wanted to be brave, and since I didn't wait until 1999, it's clearly not a Resolution. Right? Right.

XOXO,

Tessa

January, 1999

January 1st, 1999

The first day of the last year in a decade, and next year will be 2000. No more 19... how will I ever get used to *that?*

Nick called me today. I kind of chickened out on the whole asking him out thing, but he asked me to meet him, yet again. I gotta give him points for persistence. So I said yes. I'm not sure which of us was more surprised, but we're meeting at TCBY for frozen yogurt tomorrow night. I'm nervous, but I guess it's practice, right? And honestly, I have some major cravings, and I don't mean for frozen yogurt.

XOXO,

Tessa

January 3rd, 1999

Okay so... date with Nick last night. Here's how it went down.

9

I walked to TCBY, and he met me there. We had yogurt. White chocolate with Reese's for me with a heaping side of *Should I be eating in front of him? Or at all?* Ugh. Sometimes the eating disorder voices are very loud. We talked for a bit, but between my nerves and the overall lack of any sort of impression he made, I can't recall much in terms of specific dialogue.

He's cute, but not in any distinctive way. Short, medium brown hair, hazel eyes, medium build. But... he's kind of boring and thinks he's *really* funny (he's not). He was polite, though (he paid for my cone, though I offered to pay), and pleasant enough company, I suppose.

"You know, I'd really love to show you my place," he said. I licked my cone and considered. I mean, that was a pretty weak line.

"Okay. Why not?" I finally answered.

I'm being bold, right?

He has a roommate who was wearing sweats and playing a video game. The apartment was cramped and kind of a dump. I mean, definitely not worthy of showing off. Which means that yeah, that line was as much a ploy as I imagined at the time.

We went to Nick's room, which was surprisingly neat (something I find a bit off-putting since A: I am so not neat and B: I find clutter comfy and welcoming). He kissed me. It was an okay kiss. I've had better by far but also much worse. I'd call it generic, I suppose. Standard issue. Run of the mill. You get the drift.

We wound up in his bed. I wasn't really sure where things were going, but I guess I shouldn't be surprised that it involved a lot of time focused on my boobs.

I wish I could say I was into it. Instead, I was just going through the motions and only because of my whole *let's be bold, Tessa* thing. But I wasn't impressed by any of his *skills*. We didn't have sex, but he came. I didn't even come close (see what I did there?).

No cravings even remotely satisfied.

He drove me home, and that was that. I doubt I'll ever speak to him again. I certainly won't be calling him, and he got what he wanted.

However, at least I got to learn that being bold doesn't mean I hook up with someone I'm not into just because they're willing, which is honestly a lesson I should've learned from past experiences but apparently didn't.

Still, after tonight, I feel like it's finally really clicked in my twisted brain... so I'll write it off as my first attempt at being bold, and a successful one, even if I didn't get to have any orgasms.

Here's hoping for a much hotter experience the next time I hook up with someone.

XOXO,
Tessa

January 3rd, 1999

Dear Book,

I know this makes two entries in one day, but I just had to because OH MY GOD Pizza Guy called. Turns out his name is Kevin.

It was 9 pm, and I was sitting on my bed listening to Sarah McLachlan when the phone rang. I didn't recognize the number, but it was a Cranford number, so I answered.

"Hey, is this Tessa?" asked an unfamiliar voice.

"Yeah. Who is this?"

"Hi, this is Kevin. Oh, I'm the Domino's delivery guy. You slipped me your number last week."

Inside, I squealed... but I kept my cool somehow.

"Oh, hey Kevin! Nice to put a name to the face!" Ugh.

11

Did I really say that? How fucking pathetic can you get?

"I hope you don't mind me calling this late."

I told him it was fine. The truth is, I'm a total night owl, so it was still pretty early for me.

"So, I wondered if you wanted to meet up for coffee or something one night," he says.

UHM YEAH. Hell yeah. Fuck yeah!

"That would be cool," I said.

And then, the bombshell.

"I assume you know I'm married. I mean, I figured you saw the ring."

Fuck me.

Yeah, I saw the ring. It looked nothing like a wedding ring. It's thick and clunky and kind of looks like a class ring or what I've always imagined people mean when they say a signet ring. I thought maybe it was a family crest.

I HIT ON A MARRIED GUY, and HE CALLED ME.

Oy vey.

"Oh," I said. "Actually I noticed the ring, but I didn't realize it was a wedding ring."

"Yeah, well, my wife and I are having some problems right now."

Gee, you think? Even if she doesn't know it, you're clearly having "problems" if you're married and calling the chick who slipped you her number with your delivery tip.

"Oh. I see," I said. I felt kind of dumbfounded. I finally get up the nerve to hit on a guy for the first time since being rejected by the first guy I ever asked out when I was 12 (he later dated one of my best friends), and he's **fucking married**. Goddamn it.

"So, what do you think? Would you like to meet up?"

I told him I needed to think it over. I mean, after all, I **am** being bold, right? Wasn't that the goal?

But does being bold mean sleeping with another woman's husband?

Do I want to be *that* woman? The *other* woman?

I'd be lying if said there isn't a little voice whispering, *do it*... because there's something so elicit about it that, well, it sorta turns me on. Okay, maybe more than sort of. It just makes it seem so dangerous, and that apparently works for me. Who knew? But can I live with myself if I cross that line? That isn't something I can undo when I wake up and realize I may have just ended a marriage or at least contributed to one ending.

That's not just something you shrug off the way you do when some stupid guy you're not really into makes out with you badly, and yet, for some idiotic reason, you still let him jerk off on your tits, ya know?

I have to sleep on this one.

More Soon,

Tessa

January 5th, 1999

Well, Dear Book... I went out with Kevin tonight.

We met up at the Barnes & Noble in Clark, near where I work, since it has a Starbucks inside. I'm sure the fact that it's a few towns over from where he lives helped, too.

Since I was at work all day, I had to change in the bathroom after. I wasn't going in my dirty, toddler-stained work "uniform," which consists of khaki knit pants and a polo shirt with the center's logo. I had on a long skirt, my black suede platform sneakers, and a dark-red sweater with a scoop neck that showed off some of my ample cleavage, which is one of the few things I've ever been comfortable showing off about my body. It's a look that is comfortable and casual but also trendy and cute, which I'd like to pretend I don't care about, but when you're fat with huge feet, finding clothes and shoes that are even remotely trendy and cute is such a nightmare that once in a while it's just nice to feel like you've nailed it. I put on some quick makeup, but I didn't have time for much more than a bit of blush, a swipe of dark-red lipstick, and mascara.

Still, I felt pretty good... until I walked by a window that reflected my full body back to me. Then I felt fat, ugly, and shitty. Ugh.

I reminded myself I was meeting up with a guy who chose to call me and that he did so knowing full well that I love buffalo wings with extra bleu cheese and bacon-cheeseburger pizza, since he's been delivering it to me for going on a year.

Then I heard my conscience whisper, *yes and he's fucking married.*

Kevin showed up, and my first thought was "Wow, he looks *good.*" He's probably about 5'10" and has a medium build. His floppy, dark brown hair is always slightly messy, which I find endearing. He was wearing jeans and a dark-blue sweater that made his eyes an almost midnight blue. I had that fluttery feeling I get whenever I'm attracted to someone and thought to myself, *I'm in big trouble here.*

We sat down. He got us drinks (white chocolate mochas - my favorite).

"So," I began a little tentatively before I decided to just lay it all out there, "Why did you call me if you're, well... married."

"I don't know. I swear I've never done anything like this before."

Yeah, sure you haven't, whispered my conscience.

"Well, that makes two of us," I replied. "I really did not know you were married. I'd never have slipped you my number if I'd realized. Your, uh, ring doesn't look like a wedding band," I pointed out, maybe a little defensively.

He glanced down at his ring. I took a better look at it

and felt vindicated. No one would automatically assume it was a wedding ring. It was yellow gold with a lot of black enamel and had a symbol of some sort in the round center.

"Yeah, I guess that's fair. It belonged to my wife's grandfather, and her grandmother wanted her to give it to me at our wedding."

Guess my thoughts about it weren't too far off the mark after all.

"So, if you've never done this, I mean had coffee with another woman who was interested in you, then I assume you've never, uhm..."

"Cheated?" he interjected.

"Well, yeah."

He was quiet, which had me wondering how much of what he'd told me so far was believable, but then again, the fact that he called at all had me wondering even before we met up.

"No," he finally said. "Not since we got married."

AHA!

"But before?"

"Not on my wife. The girlfriend I had before her, though. Just once, but it was a mistake, and I knew it. I ended things with both of them shortly after because I didn't think I'd been fair to either of them. The woman I cheated with didn't know I had a girlfriend, and she wanted more, but I figured if she found out I'd cheated, she'd change her mind on that, and she did."

"I can't say I blame her," I said. To his credit, he looked down and blushed a bit.

He seemed like a fairly decent person, so what the fuck was he doing here with me now that he was *actually* married?

He finally nodded in agreement and took a long sip of his coffee. Then he looked at me quizzically.

"But yet, here I am. Married and having coffee with another woman. A beautiful woman who slipped me her

15

number one night. Just her number and her name with no note. No one's ever done anything quite that bold," *he used my word!*, "before. I mean, not with me, anyway. I guess I just had to call you to find out what you were all about."

Beautiful? He did just call me beautiful, right? He must have because my face felt warm, and I am sure I blushed furiously.

"I didn't know quite how bold I was being. I mean, since I didn't realize you were married. But I, uhm, I made myself this promise after Christmas that I was going to start to take more chances. I wanted to feel like I was really **living** my life and not merely existing in it. You were the first step in that experiment. I've had, uhm... well... I've had a crush on you since the first time you delivered to us, and I finally decided to be brave and act on it."

I paused, not sure what to say next. I picked up my coffee and took a small sip. Even with the syrup, it was bitter on my tongue, but I managed not to make a face. The truth is, I am not much of a coffee-drinker. I prefer tea, which I've always found fairly hilarious since my initials spell out TEA (Tessa Elizabeth Alexander). But I digress.

"I debated if I should even meet you. Well, you know that since I didn't say yes right away," I added, feeling a little awkward (or in other words, feeling like I normally do in any social situation with someone new, and especially if that social situation is also a date).

"I'm glad you decided to," Kevin said softly. He reached forward and lightly rubbed his thumb along the side of my hand. I fought off a shiver, unsure if it was one of disgust or arousal, but to be perfectly honest, I think it was likely a mix. I mean, my god, he's really good looking and so my type. And he called me beautiful. And bold.

But he's married, whispered my pesky conscience, yet again.

16

I pulled my hand back, crossed my arms, and arched an eyebrow at him, though I have no idea if that was visible behind my glasses.

"I'm not sure if I'm glad I decided to come," I replied honestly. "You have a wife, Kevin."

He sighed deeply and leaned back.

"I know. I know I shouldn't be here. I... it's hard to explain without sounding like that stereotypical bastard about to cheat on his wife, but we haven't been living like a married couple for about six months now."

"What does that even mean?"

I tried to ignore the slight quickening I felt in my belly at the idea he was "about to cheat" with *me*.

"Kelly - that's her name - stopped sleeping in our bedroom. She moved into the guest room. First, it was for just one night. We'd had a fight - over money, mainly, since as you might imagine, I don't exactly make big bucks as a pizza delivery guy - and she was pissed, but so was I. She's the one who's high maintenance, getting her hair and nails done regularly, even when money is tight. I'd forgotten to tell her about a bill, and when she went to get her nails done, her card was declined. She was 'humiliated beyond belief,' she said."

"But I figured it would blow over. At first, I thought it had, but... then, one night a few weeks later, she went out with her friends. When she came home, I was out cold. The next day, she told me that she was super drunk when her friends dropped her off, and she felt crappy and wanted to spare me being woken up, so she crashed in the guest room. Only she never came back to our room. Slowly, her clothes and shit began moving in there."

"And you have no idea why?" I asked, amazed at the complete failure of communication.

How do couples get to that point? I mean, look, I sure don't have the best track record with relationships, and I can't say I've seen any that are worthy of modeling a healthy one on in the real world, but it seems like if you get married, you should be able to talk to each other about even the hardest things. I guess I'm a bit of an idealist, along with being a reluctant romantic.

"I mean, at first I wondered if maybe she'd cheated on me that night. It doesn't really seem like her, and her parents divorce shook her up pretty badly. There was no cheating she knew about, but her mom did remarry pretty fast, so I just have a hard time imagining her doing that. But she was out with her best friend that night, and Michelle hates my guts. I mean, she refused to be Kelly's maid of honor or even a bridesmaid at our wedding."

"Wow," I said. "I can't imagine not being a bridesmaid at my best friend's wedding."

"Kelly was pretty crushed by that. I still don't even know *why* Michelle hates me so much, but she didn't even come to the ceremony. She only bothered to show up at the reception. I thought maybe she was jealous because Kelly was getting married, and she didn't even have a boyfriend. And now I'm sure Kelly's told her about our money issues, and well, other shit that probably doesn't make me seem like a prize, and I think it's probably only further convinced her that Kelly could've done better."

He stopped talking and looked away. I found myself wondering about the vague "other shit" that was causing problems in his marriage.

"How long have you been married?" I asked.

"Four years, almost. We were 24 when we got married."

I just sat there, trying to absorb it all. Suddenly, I felt rather like a therapist instead of a date. People are always telling me I'm easy to talk to, so I guess it's not surprising. Given the situation, I decided I was okay with it.

"Have you tried to talk to her about it?"

"Yeah, but she shuts me down. I guess I'm feeling like there's no future if she won't even talk to me about anything, so when you gave me your number, it felt good. Just to have someone who actually wanted to be with me."

I didn't really know what to say to that. I could certainly relate to it feeling good, since I had that feeling when he'd actually called. I shifted awkwardly in my seat, tugging down my sweater before it threatened to expose any of the skin above the waistline of my skirt.

"Look," I finally said after a few minutes of silence that felt like an hour, "I can't be the other woman. I don't know what I was doing when I agreed to meet you, even just for coffee. I may want to be bold or want to feel like I'm taking chances in life, but I also don't want to be the catalyst for someone's divorce."

He looked disappointed, but he nodded.

"I kind of had a feeling," he said, with a rueful smile.

"I'm sorry, Kevin. I hope you sort things out with Kelly, but no matter what's going on, she doesn't deserve what could happen here if this goes further. Obviously, I am attracted to you, or I wouldn't have given you my number. I was flattered you called because, to be honest, I don't have the best luck with guys. Most of them aren't interested in me because..." I hesitated and felt my face getting hot, but I pushed through. "Well, because I'm fat," I blurted.

"It's their loss, then. Look, Tessa... I get that you can't go any further with this, and I respect that. You're also probably right that I should work things out with her, or at least try to before I sleep with someone else."

I raised my eyebrow again, and I guess he could see that after all because he quickly added, "Okay, so you're definitely right. But you're beautiful. Honestly. I thought so the first time I saw you. Those long, red curls and your big, brown eyes... plus, you have an amazing smile. It made me feel warm inside, which sounds really corny, but it's also just true. I always liked delivering to you. On top of that, you're smart and funny and clearly have a good heart based on tonight."

I was speechless. No one had ever said anything even

remotely like that to me (not about my appearance at least). Not only that, but he didn't do what most guys (and even female friends) did when I said I was fat. He didn't say, "Oh, you're not fat!" or "Don't talk about your-self that way." I hate that because it's such an obvious lie when I am *very* clearly actually fat.

But Kevin... he didn't mention it at all. I find a guy who thinks I am beautiful and didn't feel a need to even mention my weight (or the size of my boobs), and he has to be FUCKING MARRIED?!?

My life sucks.

I did the right thing, and I know it. I don't know what will happen with him and his wife, but I'm not going to sleep with someone else's husband. I just can't. It's not who I am, and I don't want it to be.

But you can damn sure bet that before I fall asleep to-night, I am *so* fantasizing about what might've been if only my moral compass hadn't shown me the right way. No one gets hurt when I fantasize about being the bad girl that a teensy part of me wishes I could have been.

Now, if you'll excuse me... I have some orgasms wait-ing to be had.

XOXO,
Tessa

January 6th, 1999

Dearest Book,

I'm a mess tonight. I rejoined Fat Fighters. I was 411 lbs, which is worse than I expected, even though I said I weighed around 400 lbs earlier. The truth is, I wrote that thinking it was a high estimate, and that I could be happy when it was much lower. Why does it even matter so much? It's not like I've ever been thin. Well, okay technically I was briefly thin when I was about 10 to 11 years old and had been on a diet for two years, but no one ever said I was thin or normal, and the kids still said I was fat. Hell, my family still said I was fat. I was 5'2" and 98 lbs at that point, which for the record is technically underweight on the BMI charts. But I've been over 300 lbs since I was a teenager.

I look at catalogs and see women wearing clothes that are meant to fit me, but they're all so small, and frankly, the clothes look too big on them (they probably are). Calling them "plus size" is insulting to those of us who actually wear those clothes.

So, now I am back to tracking all of my food as of tomorrow. I have "suggested menu ideas" from Fat Fighters. They look okay, I guess.

Right now, I'm eating donuts and ice cream. Might as well live it up tonight, while I can, right?

Wish me luck. I'm gonna need it.

XOXO,

Tessa

January 7th, 1999

I got through today okay, despite the Fat Fighters program being in full effect. I feel giddy and happy that I succeeded, even if it's only the first day. I mean, there's that whole *a journey begins with a single step* quote (or something like it) that's on so many inspirational posters or calendars and shit, right?

But I had a fight with Vanessa at work. I hate when we fight, and since we work together now, that makes it even worse. I was stressed because the new assistant they hired for me flaked, and they put Van in to cover for her. I don't think she'll be coming back, because she didn't even call until 2 hours past the start of her shift. I'm pretty sure Aimee (our director) is firing her. Aimee is sweet and a bit of a softy, but she's also no pushover, so I imagine Sandra is done-for after today's stunt.

Sandra is the seventh assistant teacher I've had in six months. The best one was Alison, but she was temporary because she was going back to college after the summer. Then there was Marina, who was also really good, but she had a family crisis and moved back to Kansas after two months. The others aren't even worth mentioning because none of them wanted the job. All of them had attitude problems, and they didn't last. Two got fired; the others quit.

Anyway, all of this was weighing on my mind, and I was frustrated. I am sure I was snippy because when I'm stressed like that, I can be a bit quick to snap at people who don't deserve it, so I know I bear at least part of the blame for the fight.

But then Vanessa brought up her boyfriend, Pete, and accused me of not liking him, and I guess insinuated I was jealous because she's with someone and I'm not.

Uh, wait, what? How does that relate to what was going on at all? I mean, yeah I told her about my recent shitty experiences but not today and not during work. I mean, I have to be honest. I don't like Pete. I don't trust him. I know he wants to sleep with me, which is an unusually cocky thing for me to say, but I can just tell. He's made some comments like calling me sexy (when Van wasn't there naturally), which I found utterly inappropriate for my best friend's boyfriend, and I've caught him staring at my boobs more than once. I've never pointed any of it out to Van, because I'm pretty sure she'd either laugh it off or get mad at me, although, come to think of it, it's probably both.

But anyway, I just stopped, bleach bottle in my hand (I was wiping down the table after lunch).

"What the hell are you talking about?" I asked in an angry whisper (the kids were napping, and there was no way I was gonna risk waking them up).

She just rolled her eyes and said, "You know exactly what I mean." Then she left for her lunch break.

The afternoon was so full of tension that my neck hurts, and I have a fucking headache. I know I owe her an apology for snapping at her when I was stressed about Sandra not showing up, but I'm still kind of baffled by where the fight went.

She's my ride to work tomorrow, and as mad as she is at me right now, I know she won't blow me off. So I guess we'll talk then. Hopefully, we'll both be calmer, and we can work through it.

For now, I think I'll distract myself by calling in to my mailbox to see if any interesting guys have left me messages.

XOXO,
Tessa

January 10th, 1999

Dear Book,

Please forgive my absence the past few days. First off, Van and I made up. She was actually upset over a fight she and Pete had had, and she admitted she was lashing out at me as a result. I apologized for my part in it but assured her I am in no way jealous of her having a boyfriend just because I don't. I left out the part where I am also not jealous because Pete seems like kind of a dick because that didn't seem conducive to us making up.

So work is okay, except they didn't fire Sandra after all, and she's a nightmare. I'm used to that, but ugh. I am seriously considering asking for a transfer to a different room. I have worked with two-year-olds for a long time, and I love them, but they are freakin' exhausting. Not having a reliable assistant doesn't help.

Anyway, I have far more interesting news. I started talking to a guy named Sebastian. He's not my usual type at all, nor do I think he is ever likely to want to meet in person. He's kind of a mystery, honestly. He's into BDSM - which I've never done - and well, let's just say the phone sex has been enlightening. I'm not sure this is something I'd ever want to do on a regular basis. He called it a "life-style" as opposed to "dabbling," and as I don't know any better, I'll go with his terms.

The thing is, if someone had asked me, I'd probably have said I would be submissive, but Sebastian is submissive, and he wanted a "mistress," so I decided to give it a try. I told him I had no idea what I was doing, but he seemed even more turned on by the fact that I was willing to be adventurous with him that way.

It's easy enough to say these kinds of things over the phone, but I doubt if I could ever do it in person. Yesterday, I told him to put a rubber band around his wrist and to snap it every time he thought about me today. I don't know what made me think of that, aside from possibly a poem I read called "Bracelet: To Julia," in a poem-a-day book I bought with my Christmas gift card. It's from a poet I'd never heard of named Robert Herrick, but there's something rather sensual and suggestive about it, and yet it's also very romantic:

Why I tie about thy wrist,
Julia, this my silken twist?
For what other reason is't,
But to shew thee how in part
Thou my pretty captive art?
But thy bond-slave is my heart;
'Tis but silk that bindeth thee,
Knap the thread and thou art free;
But 'tis otherwise with me;
I am bound, and fast bound so,
That from thee I cannot go;
If I could, I would not so.

I don't know who Julia was to him, but something about this poem made me think of Sebastian and the whole BDSM thing. I have no idea if that's how it was intended, but the idea that he's tying a bracelet of silk around her wrist to show her that she's his captive, and yet he's really her captive because she's stolen his heart... that just seems really romantic and hot in a *pull-my-hair-and-spank-me* kind of way. Now, obviously that's assuming Julia wasn't actually his captive. I guess I should find out more about this dude, but still, as someone who writes poems and stories, I really appreciated the cadence of this poem, and I definitely found it alluring.

A rubber band is far less sensual than a silken thread, but hey... we work with what we can, right? At any rate, he seemed to love the idea, though a little voice in my head wondered if he wasn't just messing with me. Like he was gonna hang up the phone and start laughing his ass off and tell all of his friends about this. Oh anxiety, my constant companion, always making me doubt myself.

Part of me wonders why I am talking to a guy I have no intention of ever meeting, even if he wanted to (which, like I said, I doubt he would). I mean, he has a really sexy voice, so there's that, but also there's something about the anonymity of it all that is allowing me to explore a side of myself I'd never even considered might exist. So in and of itself, that feels kind of brazen and fulfilling.

I wish I could be as confident in the real world as I am on the phone. I feel like phone-me is usually representative of my true self... she's playful, funny, flirtatious and, well, free. In person, though, I either clam up and say nothing or I ramble on and on and can't find the damn off switch.

Sometimes (okay, most of the time) I think it's that on the phone I can be the "thin" version of myself. I'm not trapped under the fat that everyone sees and judges (and everyone includes me). Don't get me wrong; I don't lie to the guys that I talk to about what I look like. Well, not anymore. I did it once, thinking I'd never meet him, and then he wanted to meet. *Sure, because he thought I was hot and thin.* Obviously, I couldn't meet him, since I'd lied, so I just told him no and stopped talking to him, but since then, I've always said I was "full-figured" because "fat," while accurate, feels like I'm insulting myself, and let's face it, people are gonna be even less likely to talk to me than they already are.

Still, despite making it clear that I am not anything even close to thin or average sized, you'd be shocked by how many guys have said idiotic things about my body not matching my voice. What the hell does that even mean? I guess I have the voice of Jessica Rabbit without the body to go with it.

I've also had guys say I was different on the phone than I was in person, which yeah, I guess I'm not shocked to hear that. The thing is, most of those guys who used that as their excuse for never calling again or for not wanting a second date (when I bother to get an answer at all) also spent time making out with me... so what gives? I wasn't the same as I was on the phone, but you still had enough of a good time to want to lock lips for twenty minutes or more?

It's so fucking frustrating. So while I do think there's

26

something I can learn through this phone "friendship" with Sebastian, the truth is that I'm also feeling a bit overwhelmed and intimidated by meeting people again. Why can't I meet a person the normal way? At a party or at work?

Being fat inevitably puts me firmly in the friends-only lane while I watch friends of mine date the guys I liked (and yes, they usually knew I liked said guy). Just once, it would be nice if a guy I met could just like me. ALL of me. All 399 lbs of me (as of my second Fat Fighters meeting). All of me, quirks, and anxieties, and insecurities, and stretch marks.

I guess when even I struggle to like how I look, it's not shocking that potential romantic partners would, too. I know I would date a fat person if they made me laugh and they were cute, smart, and kind.

Sigh. Why is it all so hard and complicated?

That is why I end up hiding in my room having phone sex with guys I'll most likely never meet rather than finding people to actually date. There is no shortage of guys on Voice Personals who want to have phone sex with me, and while some of them would be happy to also have real sex with me, very few would ever want their friends to know about it.

I can't say the idea of being some guy's secret lover is exactly appealing, especially when the "secret" involves him being too asshamed of me to want anyone to see him with me. Hah, I accidentally wrote asshamed. I meant ashamed, but you know what? It works because they are asses who *should* feel ashamed. But not of ME.

I say that and mean it, but then that evil voice whispers, *but why not? You're ashamed of you, too.*

I guess I'm just full of self-loathing tonight.

And on that note, more soon. Hopefully, I'll be in a better mood next time.

XOXO,

Tessa

January 24th, 1999

Dear Book,

I know it's been a while, but I've been busy! I got a promotion at work. It wasn't the one I wanted, but it does mean an extra thirty cents an hour. I know it's pitiful. I also formally transferred to the infant room. There are eight babies in total, and I have a great co-teacher. There's an aide who comes in to help for a few hours a day (and covers lunch breaks). I am loving it. My boss thought I'd be bored in a week, but she's wrong. The youngest baby is just six weeks old, and the oldest is 10 months, and once he starts walking, he'll be transferred to the older infant/pre-toddler room.

There's just something magical about having these tiny, little lives so dependent on us and so trusting. I fall more in love with them every day, especially when they fall asleep on me. I have a knack for getting an overtired infant to fall asleep. Jan (the aide) said that's because they like the "pillows" of my boobs haha... but then again, both she and my co-caregiver have small boobs and have a bitch of a time getting a kid to fall asleep, so maybe she's not wrong.

Work has been really great, overall. I'm happy with that part of my life, at least.

Dieting has been... well, frustrating. I lost 20 lbs in the first two weeks, but then it stopped. I didn't change anything, either. I'm still active at work, even though it's different in the infant room. I'm still lifting babies all day, getting up and down off the floor, changing diapers (every freaking hour, unless they are asleep - center rules), so I can't figure out what the problem is.

The worst part is going into Fat Fighters meetings to get weighed when you haven't lost weight. The person doing the weighing is a member who has reached their goal weight and maintained it for a set period of time. It's always a woman (I've yet to see a single man in a Fat Fighters meeting who worked for them), and she always gives me a look that says, *I know you did something bad this week,* but then she says some stupid platitude about plateaus (yeah, but it's not even a damn month) and pretends like she isn't silently judging me when it's so fucking clear that she is.

Trust me, lady. You aren't judging me any harder than I am judging myself.

But I am trying to resist the temptation to just say *fuck it* and eat whatever's in the fridge. It's easier said than done, especially given my history.

I first remember binge eating when I was maybe 3 or 4. I can't say what triggered it, but given my family's insanity, I'd guess maybe my parents forgot to feed me lunch or something, or my father stole my dinner from my plate (he did that a lot), but I ate half a package of cold hot dogs in what felt like five minutes.

That was the first in what would become a long line of binge-eating episodes. When I was a teenager, it morphed into bulimia, except I couldn't force myself to throw up. Not from lack of trying, mind you. I did plenty of trying, even employing various methods I'd heard other bulimics discuss after I spent weeks in Pleasant Pines psychiatric hospital in the eating disorder unit. I could just never make it happen, which is a good thing. However, I did have the lesser-known, non-purging type of bulimia. I'd binge, then restrict my food intake drastically for days while also often over-exercising to make up for the binges.

Sometimes, I have moments of thinking dieting isn't all that different from those days, except I'm not binging (at least not so far). I exercise so I can eat more, I restrict my food, and I try to make up for days when I've eaten more than I think I should have (even though it was within my daily allotment for Fat Fighters). In these moments, I wonder what I'm doing this for, but then my leader says something like *nothing tastes as good as thin feels,* and oh, how I want to know that feeling. Fuck, it feels better than chocolate tastes? Because chocolate tastes pretty damn amazing, and *technically* I've been thin and didn't even fucking know it. No one else did, either.

So I mean, if that's what thin feels like... well, then it doesn't really feel all that different from fat, does it?

Of course, I'd be able to shop in any store if I were thin, instead of just Lane Bryant or The Avenue, and I wouldn't worry about restaurants having only booths and no tables. Things my thin friends who whine about being fat can't possibly understand, because oh yeah, they *aren't* actually fat and never have been. They've never been through any of the humiliation I have.

Like when in high school I lied about my weight on my cap and gown form for graduation and then panicked that my gown wouldn't fit and had to tearfully confess to my favorite teacher about it. Or the time I thought I'd gotten stuck in a turnstile on the Philly subway. It turned out I had just caught my bag in one of the spokes, but still, I had a moment of pure, total panic because I had definitely had to squeeze through it (sideways, no less) to fit.

They can't understand that every time I go anywhere new, I'm terrified about seating arrangements. Will the place have sturdy chairs? Will they have arms? Will desks in a classroom have that stupid flip-up desk top that's supposed to lay flat in front of you, except mine is always crooked, and that's with me holding my breath and sucking my belly in as much as I can. They don't know how much that type of body contortion hurts by the end of the day.

I'm so fed up and tired of fighting my body all the time and never coming out ahead. Just for once, I'd like it to WORK when I try to lose weight. I'm doing it all right, but people don't even believe me about it.

Okay, enough about that. I can't discuss it anymore, because I'm getting all anxious.

So dating... well, there's not a lot to report. I went on a few dates that were all duds for one reason or another. A guy named Jonathan is into me sexually but isn't really romantically interested (at least he's honest about it). I'm not into him anyway, frankly. He's not my type, and he's a mama's boy, which is something that I do not find at all appealing. It just always makes me think that if I get involved with a guy who dotes on his mom that way, and she hates me, he's going to side with her and not me. Maybe that's paranoid, but it's how I feel.

I called a different service. It was like a party line with multiple people talking all at once. It can be kind of chaotic, but I met a girl named Scarlet, and we have amazing phone chemistry. No one knows I'm bisexual aside from Van and Nathaniel (my little brother) who found my Playboy magazine stash once. He likes to hold it over my head as something he's going to blab about to our parents. Frankly, I don't think either of them would give a flying fuck, so I don't worry about it overly much. My dad's sister is gay, and my mom has gay friends, but Nathaniel's so homophobic that I'm sure that it doesn't occur to him that our parents might not be that way. Pfft. They were like hippies born just a little too late to truly qualify.

The only problem is that Scarlet lives in Boston. Still, we've been talking a lot and having a lot of fun. She's a few years older than I am and also bisexual. She's (supposedly) a natural redhead, which is such a major thing for me. When I was 19, I woke up from a dream because I'd had an orgasm in my sleep, and the dream was about this unbelievably sexy redhead going down on me. I had first dyed my hair red at 13, but that dream had me doing it again just because I wanted to feel sexy, and I thought maybe that would help (I guess it kind of did).

31

Scarlet and I have been talking every night. I know I should be focusing on local people, but I don't know how to meet women locally. Voice Personals for women seeking women isn't free, and I can't afford it. I don't have a credit card, anyway, which is required. I'm so sick of dating men. It's just been going so badly for so long. I've also never dated a woman. Hell, until Scarlet, I never even considered it. I always thought that I was only sexually attracted to women, but that to be emotionally satisfied, I'd have to be with a man.

Suddenly, I am realizing that's not the case at all, which has me again considering coming out to my mom. I never saw a need when all I imagined was hooking up with another chick. So far, the furthest I've gotten is some serious kissing... which may have happened to go below the neck. That was with Dara, a chick I met at summer camp when we were both 14. We somehow wound up confessing that we were curious about being intimate with another girl, but it wasn't anything even remotely serious, although it was seriously hot. We both wound up coming just from playing with each other's nipples. Oh, did I mention that it was a Christian summer camp? Yeah, we'd have been in some serious shit if we'd been caught. It was during the bonfire, which was always held on the last night of camp. People would get all cozy under sleeping bags, and sometimes there would be a few tents. There was always a lot of hooking up happening, and the camp counselors had to have some clue because they were all previous campers and only in their late teens or early twenties, with few exceptions. I'm sure they had been doing the same thing just a few years before, but still that wouldn't have stopped them from acting all holier-than-thou if they'd caught anyone... and especially two girls!

So, Dara and I got there early and snagged a tent. Then, after dark, when the others were sleeping and the fire created dancing shadows on the inside of the tent, we began to kiss. Dara looked luminous in the dim light. I remember glimpses of her soft breasts, nipples hard in the chilly night air. I'll never forget my first impression of a girl's lips upon mine. I'd only kissed two boys, but this felt completely different, so soft and gentle. I remember thinking that it was like making out with a marshmallow, which sounds really weird, but trust me... it felt really, really good.

I think the main reason we didn't take it further is that we were so scared of getting caught, and the fact that we came without completely removing any clothes was fairly impressive (at least to us), but the fear of getting caught also made things so much more intense.

Unfortunately, I haven't had another chance to kiss a girl since, and now with me and Scarlet all hot and heavy on the phone, I can't help but think about it all. I doubt I'll ever meet Scarlet in person, but I definitely would be open to it.

Okay, falling asleep. Time for bed.

XOXO,

Tessa

February

February 1st, 1999

So, tomorrow is my birthday, and I get to celebrate it by... drumroll please... being sick as hell with strep throat! Woohoo! Oh, wait. I guess on the plus side, it means I'm not working for at least two days this week. And it's early enough in the year that I still have paid sick days (they won't last long).

To celebrate, my mom let me get whatever takeout I wanted for dinner. I went with Chinese so I could get wonton soup, which I figured would help my throat, and it's one of the foods they tell us is a good menu choice for Fat Fighters.

I am not getting a cake, because I don't need the temptation. But I did eat a fortune cookie tonight, and it had the weirdest fucking fortune I've ever seen:

*The rubber bands are heading
in the right direction.*

Oh. Uhm, sure. I mean, I have a fever, but I'm not delusional enough to make that shit up. If I were still talking to Sebastian, we might have a laugh at this. I stopped talking to him, because he started to get weirdly possessive. I mean, it was just some phone sex, and sure, I'm good, but c'mon. It's not like it's real.

Of course, I say that even though Scarlet told me last night that she thinks she's in love with me, and I have to admit that it made me feel pretty damn warm and fuzzy. She also sent me the cutest birthday card and a bracelet (because I'd read her that poem I'm obsessed with) so I'd think of her often... as if I have a choice!

I also talked to a guy a few days ago that might have meet-up potential. Scarlet and I have been open about the fact that, given the distance, we can't expect each other to stay single, or not be with anyone else, but the deal is that we have to tell each other. After last night's call, I just don't know if I can do that to her.

Yet, I also know I have the right to have a real relationship, and right now, that's not an option with Scarlet. As it turns out, it probably never will be. No one in her family knows she isn't straight, and they are apparently very religious and against the idea of same-sex couples. She's close to her family and doesn't want to hurt them. I said, "but what about hurting yourself?" She said that she **thinks** she could be happy with the right man, but then she confessed she's not really sure if she's bisexual or a lesbian.

Sigh.

So given that, I don't think there's any hope for anything real with her, which seriously sucks because honestly, I think I could fall in love with her, and I wouldn't give a flying fuck what my family had to say about it. I am not putting their happiness over my own, and if that makes me some kind of selfish bitch, oh well. I think family should be happy for you if you're lucky enough to find love... whether it's heterosexual or not.

On that depressing note, I'm gonna to try to sleep

through this stupid sore throat. I am glad I can sleep in tomorrow, at least. Silver linings and shit.

XOXO,
Tessa

February 10th, 1999

Well, things with Scarlet have ended. Two nights ago, I told her that I thought I was falling in love with her. She told me she loved me - again. I thought maybe there was some way to move forward after all.

I told her I could take vacation time and come up to Boston to meet up with her. She sounded really excited about it, and we were talking about what we'd do and where she'd take me (since I've never been there). It suddenly seemed like this was possible.

But she just called me, in tears. Apparently she decided to test the waters with her family by telling her older sister. It didn't go well.

"If you don't end it with that girl tonight, I am going to have to tell Mom and Dad. I will immediately stop allowing you to see Jenny and Adam (Scarlet's niece and nephew), because I will not let them grow up around you if that's the way you choose to live your life."

Oh. I'm sorry, but what the fuck? Why can't people just be happy for their loved ones when they find someone they care about?

I feel truly awful. I let my guard down and started to really care about her, but most of all, I feel terrible for her because she told me tonight that she's had sex with two men and hated it. Passionately. She always acted like she was into guys the same amount until she confessed she might be a lesbian, and now this. So, I really don't think she's bisexual at all, and yet if she wants her family in her life, she has to pretend to be something she's not.

She adores her niece and nephew, and I understand her love for them. They're just innocent children being used by a parent in a way I find despicable, but I'm feeling pretty heartbroken over it at the moment, and I can't stop crying. I honestly think I'm crying more for her than for me.

I'll respect her decision, even if I personally can't fully understand wanting these people who'd treat her this way in her life.

I guess it's time to meet Ryan. I've still been talking to him casually, but he knew I was "sort of seeing someone." He just didn't know the details.

It's hard to think of meeting anyone else right now even though I do like him, at least so far. Who knows when we meet in person if he'll be horrified by my fatness? Or at least too ashamed of it to let anyone see me with him.

Ugh. Okay, I'm going to cry myself to sleep now. Guess the rubber bands weren't heading in the right direction after all.

XOXO,
Tessa

February 14th, 1999

Have I mentioned that I despise Valentine's Day? Because I do.

But tonight... tonight was actually a pretty good Valentine's. I met up with Ryan for the second time.

I didn't plan to meet him at all, or at least not yet. I was still upset over what happened with Scarlet (or I guess what didn't happen), but she called me the day after she ended things, and we talked for over an hour.

"I don't want you to feel like you can't move on. I know you've been talking to that guy... Robert?" She said.

"Ryan," I replied, through tears because hearing her voice again just hurt. I really got invested, too much and too fast. Damn stupid romantic streak.

"Okay, well. Please do this for me. When this call ends, promise me you'll call him. Please?" Her voice broke on the final please, and I started sobbing in earnest.

"Okay," I said quietly.

We talked for a few more minutes after that, and when we hung up, I kept my promise.

Ryan surprised me by asking if I was free the following night, and keeping my word to Scarlet, I told him yes.

We met up at Barnes & Noble (I do love that place, and since it's walking distance from work - and public - it's ideal for these things). He told me he'd be wearing a red sweater, so he was pretty easy to find.

He's seriously adorable. He's not what I'd call fat, though I'm sure others might. I'd say he's like... I don't know... a teddy bear sounds so lame. Let's go with cuddly. He's about 6'2", and I rarely date tall guys (I'm 5'6"), but on him, it didn't feel, I don't know... overpowering? Formidable? He has dimples, and his hair is somewhere between red and brown. His eyes are this cool color that I don't even know how to describe. Sort of like a greyish green.

He was so incredibly easy to talk to, and before I knew it, I had explained the entire Scarlet thing to him. He didn't do the gross thing most guys do when they find out I am bisexual, which is to get all hot and bothered and ask stupid questions or make cracks about pillow fights in underwear... or worse, ask if I was into threesomes (for the record, I'd totally be open to it under the right circumstances - but the second I reveal my sexuality is definitely not the time to ask!!!).

He just listened, and then he explained that he broke up with his girlfriend of five years about six months ago. She got a job transfer and wanted him to go with her, but he realized that neither of them was invested enough to give up their dreams for their relationship.

It was just refreshing to be able to be so open and honest with someone. We connected, though I wasn't sure if it was just as friends, at first.

And then he kissed me goodnight.

Oh. My. God.

The boy can KISS. Like, goosebumps kinda kissing. I was so freakin' turned on. By just a KISS.

So, when he asked me if I had plans for Valentine's Day, I said no in a freakin' heartbeat. It's a Sunday, which meant we could spend most of the day together, and that's exactly what we did.

We started off with lunch at The Rustic Mill. I had my favorite (chicken salad on toasted sourdough, topped with cheddar and bacon) and didn't fucking worry about Fat Fighters at all for once. It was a relief, if I am honest. Not to mention, I was comfortable eating in front of him, which is miraculous. When I was in the worst of my eating disorder, I couldn't handle eating in front of anyone, ever. All I did was binge in secret. So when I am able to eat in front of someone I just met, without worrying that it might make them think bad things about me or my body, or that they might lecture me with *should you really be eating that*, it's a big deal for me.

He held my hand across the table while we waited for our food, and he'd brought me a single red rose. I've never, ever gotten flowers on Valentine's Day before (in fact, I've only gotten flowers twice ever). We talked about favorite books (my current is Judy Blume's *Summer Sisters*, which I've read three times since it came out last year), movies, music... and it was all so natural and relaxed.

We had talked about going to the movies, but there

was nothing good playing (what is with movies so far this year, ugh?). I considered *She's All That*, but I'm so tired of the idea that girls who are really beautiful (and they don't even hide it well) are in need of being made over to impress, well, anyone... or that anyone needs to be made over to impress anyone for that matter.

So, when I told him that I finally saw *Breakfast At Tiffany's* last year and loved it, he suggested renting it and going to his house. What the hell... I said yes.

Honestly? I can't lie. I *totally* wanted to sleep with him.

And I totally did.

It was fucking fabulous. It was the best sex of my entire life. Yeah, okay, I haven't had much sex in my entire life, but still. Until tonight, sex with myself was a fuck of a lot better than any I'd had with another person.

First off, Ryan lives alone, which isn't something I've found common in my dating experiences. Maybe it's because he's a bit older; he's 28. But even the guys I've dated his age lived with their mothers or roommates.

He rents a cute little house in Scotch Plains, which is also cool because he's really nearby.

His decor is eclectic, which I dig. He has this gorgeous sleigh bed, and I've always loved those so much. Just the idea that I was about to have sex in a sleigh bed got me hot. What can I say? I'm a sucker for cute furniture, apparently.

I was really nervous, because it wasn't fully dark yet, and of course I was feeling self-conscious about my body, especially my belly and flat ass... but he put me at ease really fast. Or at least he distracted me.

He began kissing me. It started off slow and gentle, until I nipped his bottom lip. I couldn't help myself. He has these soft, full lips that are just perfect for kissing, and as it turns out, everything else.

His eyes darkened. Maybe it was just the setting sun, and I've certainly read too many romance novels, but I swear they became a darker green. He pulled my hair out of its tie and grabbed it at the nape of my neck, pulling my mouth to his.

God, it was just all so fucking intense and hot.

I dug my nails into his back, and he began to slowly undress me. I hate that I can't find sexy lingerie in my size, and I started to feel self-conscious about my boring-as-hell nude bra and granny panties with flowers, but he didn't seem to notice or mind whatsoever, and before long, I forgot to feel anything but amazing.

He pushed me down onto that awesome bed, which was even more comfortable than it looked. His weight on top of me as he kissed me was making me crazy, and I could feel his erection against my thigh.

"You're too dressed," I whispered. I desperately wanted to feel his body against mine, which was now fully naked in the dying light.

He just laughed a deep, husky laugh and said, "you'll have to wait," and then... he began kissing down my neck, spending a generous amount of time on my nipples before he slipped a hand between my thighs and began to massage my clit. I came almost instantly. I've never come that fast with anyone else, except myself.

He followed that with a trail of kisses down my body, and yes, I began feeling self-conscious again when he got to my belly, but yet again, he quickly made me forget those feelings. His tongue languished around my belly button. I never knew a belly button could be an erogenous zone until tonight.

I had my hands in his lush hair, and I can't deny I was pushing his head down. He obliged, and I wound up coming several more times before he'd let me take off his clothes.

This is where I am weird, because although I most definitely love sex with men (or at least I did tonight), I don't find their naked bodies all that, uhm, appealing. I much prefer the sight of a naked woman.

So you're not going to hear me talk about how beautiful Ryan's cock is, because to be perfectly honest, I've yet to see one I'd call beautiful. However, his was attached to his amazingly-skilled body, which *definitely* made my night beautiful.

I was dying to have him inside me, and I couldn't take it anymore. I just gasped, "oh my god, Ryan... please fuck me."

I have literally never been so blunt or brazen in my entire life.

And oh, did he ever. We had sex three times. THREE TIMES in as many hours. I don't even know how many orgasms I had.

Needless to say, I am feeling incredibly satisfied and impressed with myself. I mean, hey, I said I wanted to have fun this year, right? Well, I'd say I accomplished that and then some today.

I have no idea where it's going to go from here. I don't really care, either, which is luxurious. If he never called me again, I'd still remember this night fondly for the rest of my life.

XOXO,

Tessa

PS. I finished writing this, and he called ten minutes later. We just finished having amazing phone sex, so I'd say it's going to go *somewhere*.

February 22, 1999

Dear Book,

It's been a busy week, but I spent all weekend with

Ryan, and yes, there was a lot of sex. It was every bit as amazing as the first time(s). In fact, even better.

I can't say I think I'll fall in love with Ryan. I am not sure why. It's like he's a great guy and an amazing listener... and god, when he looks at me, I get all weak-kneed, but it's kind of like having a best friend you just happen to fuck. A lot.

We discussed it this weekend, and he feels much the same way. Not that we don't care about one another, but just that neither of us is feeling a "romance" in a traditional sense. We can't keep our hands off each other, but we're in lust and definitely not love, or so it seems.

I'm good with this. I wasn't looking for "the one" anymore, if you recall. I just wanted to have fun.

Ryan is good for me. Not just the orgasms (though my skin has been radiant lately). No, he's great for my self-esteem.

I haven't been to a Fat Fighters meeting since late last month, and you know what? I am okay with it. I'm not feeling obsessive about everything for once in my fucking life, and I don't particularly want to ever feel that again.

Ryan and I talked about this a lot. I was telling him how when I'm with him, I stop feeling awkward and ugly. I feel beautiful and confident. He said, "that's because you are beautiful and confident," Tess.

And when he says it, I feel like I can almost believe it to be true. I at least desperately want it to be true.

So I am thinking I may not go back to Fat Fighters. I wrote that I was either going to "do something" about my weight or accept being fat. What if the "something" that I "do" happens to be accepting myself? Is that entirely batshit crazy?

I don't know if it's something I can even really pull off. I mean, I still have that desire to be thin, but at the same time, I've spent too much of my life *weighting* (see what I did there?) to live, like I didn't deserve it if I wasn't a certain weight or size.

Certainly, society does not to disabuse me of this notion. I mean, just the conversations at Fat Fighters alone constantly make it clear that if you weigh more than what's deemed "acceptable," you are somehow worth less. It's ironic that I can feel both so big and so small all at the same time, for the exact same reasons.

Anyway, I don't know. I wish I had a therapist, but it's been years since I have. I have to check my insurance to see if it covers that. Maybe I should find one.

Next weekend, Ryan and I are going away to Vermont. I took a vacation day, and we're doing two nights in a little cabin. I'm crazy excited because as silly as it might sound, I've always wanted to have sex in front of a fireplace.

He has a friend who owns a few cabins up there, and she'll be there (in a different one). Ryan - unsurprisingly - has a lot of female friends. I am glad I'm not interested in more than what we currently have because I'd have a really hard time not being jealous of them, especially since I've seen pics of a few of them, and they're all freakin' gorgeous (and *way* thinner than I am).

Yet, I don't feel jealous at all. It is kind of weird, frankly. I know he and this friend Mia have had sex before, but he said it's been quite a long time. Apparently, until very recently, Mia was in a relationship. She was even engaged, but her fiance broke her heart when he cheated on her. I think Ryan said his name was Tyler, but since he was, uhm, trying to change the subject, I'm not sure if I remember it right.

Mia is stunning, at least in the pics I've seen of her. She has these dark brown eyes with crazy long lashes and really beautiful, full lips. She's definitely not thin, and while I am sure some would call her fat, to me she has the perfect body, the kind I wish I had and just recently realized (like duh, lightbulb moment, realized) that even if I lost every extra pound on my body I'd never have. I'm simply not built that way. She has a more hourglass shape, all softness and gentle curves. She's wearing a bikini in one pic, and she's just... fucking glorious. She's exactly my type, at least physically (even if she doesn't have red hair).

As for me, I have no defined waist, a flat ass, and most of my weight is in my belly and boobs. I'm trying to come to terms with this realization that I will never have that body type, no matter what, because it suddenly feels like, *wait so even if I were thin I'd probably find reasons to hate my body because it's not what I thought it would be or should be*, but I digress.

I have to admit that I kind of felt something stir when I saw Mia's pics. I can't even really explain it. I just felt this immediate attraction when I saw her. Something in her eyes drew me and captivated me, just from a picture.

Not that I think there's a chance in hell there could ever be anything between us (as far as I know, she's straight), but if there was a chance? I'd jump all over that! Unless I hate her when I meet her, but I suspect that if Ryan likes her, I will, too. I get the impression he's fairly picky... which totally makes me sound conceited, now that I think about it. Ha! Me sounding conceited. That's a kick.

So, I'll fill you in on the details when I get back from Vermont since I don't anticipate having time to write while there. Ryan's taking me to dinner tomorrow, and I might wind up spending the night. He mentioned he could drop me at work.

Bedtime.

XOXO,
Tessa

February 23, 1999

Not Tyler. TAYLOR. Mia's fiance was another woman. It never even dawned on me to imagine a fiance of the same sex. I guess since you can't get married legally, I just didn't think that people did, but of course they do. Ceremonies matter, even if it's not legal. Honestly, the words you're saying and commitments you're making mean more than some slip of paper that makes it all official, or at least they should.

Sometimes, I feel so naive and sheltered. This is one of them. It makes me happy, though, to know that there are people out there getting engaged and having a friend perform a ceremony for them, even though it's not legally binding. I love the idea that people are saying *fuck that, I can still get married.*

I hope someday they get the legal rights heterosexual couples get because it's seriously BS. I believe that even if I were straight, I'd feel strongly about this, but I guess since it's become clear to me recently that I'm not, I could theoretically wind up with a woman. I'm thinking about it more, especially in the context of learning that Mia was engaged to another woman.

Anyway, Mia's apparently pansexual (I've seriously never heard that one before) and open to relationships with anyone she feels connected to, regardless of their gender.

Still, she's Ryan's friend. She and I have both had sex with him. I'm currently having regular sex with him.

I mean, there are just so many potential complications... and I may not even LIKE her. Just because I think she looks like some kind of fertility goddess doesn't mean she's NICE or smart or anything else positive. She could be a total bitch.

I'm pretty hung up on personality. In fact, while my friends are busy gushing over some hot actor (or actress),

I'm crushing on the character they portray instead.

So what are the odds? Even then, she'd have to be interested in ME, and I honestly cannot see that happening. She's so... gorgeous. And I'm so... *not*.

Sigh.

So much for being conceited.

XOXO,

Tessa

February 25th, 1999

Dear Book,

I found a therapist! She sounded very nice over the phone, and she takes my insurance. She's right here in Cranford, so I can walk there, and she does evening appointments, which is good since I work until 5:30 most nights.

My first session is not until April 21st at 6:30 pm, and I'm nervous but also really excited.

XOXO,

Tessa

February 26th, 1999

Okay, so I'm freaking out, and not in a happy way. I am currently hiding in a bathroom at a rest stop in Massachusetts, where we've stopped for gas and food. Ryan just told me that he called Mia to check things out for tonight, and she told him there's been a change of plans.

Apparently, the cabin Ryan and I were to stay in had a last-minute rental from a couple she's known for years, and she didn't want to turn them down. I get that, and we were staying for free as her guests since she and Ryan are friends BUT... I do not handle a sudden change of plans well.

Now we're apparently staying in the "big house" with her, and I'm having massive anxiety about spending the weekend with a stranger. Not to mention that I'm also bummed because I really wanted the time alone with Ryan, you know, for sex and stuff? Like it was going to be super romantic, and now I just feel like it's gonna be crazy awkward and weird. Or I will be, at the very least.

I'd better get back to the car, but I had to get that out before I exploded. I'm trying not to cry. Panic attacks suck.

XOXO,

Tessa

February 27th, 1999 (7:45 am)

Well, my freakout was for nothing. Mia's "big house" is uh, well, really big. I mean, you could have a family of eight here without any cramping. Ryan and I have this gorgeous room, complete with its own bathroom, deck, and even a wood-burning stove. It's not a fireplace, but it's close enough.

It's an old farmhouse that she apparently inherited from her grandparents and renovated a couple of years ago. Everything is super rustic, but also modern, and it's really gorgeous. It's not the cozy little cabin I was imagining, but it's still crazy nice.

And so is she. Mia is everything Ryan said she was.

She's charming, funny, and smart. And yeah, she's every bit as gorgeous in person, but it's even better because she has the personality to go with it, and that is so important to me.

If she wasn't so nice and generous, it would be easy to hate her. She has quite an interesting life, in addition to being beautiful and brilliant. She's from money, and in addition to the property (all three rental cabins are on the same land as this big house), she inherited a truckload (her word) of money. She's not really a materialistic person, and she liked her job - she does medical research - so she donates a lot of money and works part-time so she can also volunteer. Yeah, seriously.

She lives in NYC, in Manhattan (I've only dreamed of living there since I was 15). She's already invited me to visit her there.

I'm kind of smitten.

We had wine. I've literally never had wine until tonight - I know, I know. I wish I could say I liked it, but it was kind of bitter to me. I got a slight buzz, and it was nice to sit by the fireplace in the living room to just talk and relax.

Ryan was very touchy-feely with me all night. At first I thought that might be weird, given the history between him and Mia, but she didn't seem to be at all bothered by any of it.

When we got to our room, he built a fire in the stove, laid a bunch of pillows and blankets on the floor, and we spent about an hour just making out. Of course, we finished it with some mind blowing sex. I was trying not to be too loud because I was afraid Mia might hear, and I swear he considered that a challenge and was intentionally trying to make me crazier.

"Ryan," I gasped at one point. "Mia's going to hear, and I have to face her in the morning."

His response? To bite my nipple, which made me moan. He pushed my breasts together and sucked both nipples at once, and I basically lost it at that point. I came almost immediately, and yeah, I was *so* not quiet.

Mia **had** to have heard. I have to go down to breakfast now, and I'm kind of mortified.

XOXO,

Tessa

February 27, 1999 (12:30 pm)

"So, it sounded like you two had a good night," Mia said as she passed me the milk for my tea.

I swear, I felt myself turn 100 shades of red. She winked at me.

"It's okay, Tess... I know the things he's capable of, so I can't blame you."

Now it was Ryan's turn to blush, which I found oddly endearing. He suddenly found the newspaper very interesting.

"Anyone want some toast? I got this amazing cinnamon raisin bread from the farmer's market, yesterday," Mia continued, casually.

"Uhm, sure..." I said, flustered.

As she stood up, she put a hand on my shoulder and leaned forward. She tucked a strand of my hair behind my ear and whispered, in a husky voice that made me instantly wet, "by the way... you sound amazing when you come."

OH. MY. GOD.

I am simultaneously mortified, turned on and flattered.

Not to mention, that whole exchange was really fucking flirtatious. Or maybe I imagined it. I can't decide.

Ryan definitely didn't hear what she said, but he raised

an eyebrow at me in curiosity when she did it.

A few weeks ago, I found myself wanting Ryan in a way I've never wanted anyone before... and now... I want Mia even more.

The thing is, Mia... Mia I could fall for. I don't know how I know that with such gut certainty, but I do. She's compassionate. She's witty. She's sassy.

She's dangerous.

This is crazy. This is so not my life.

Yet, here I am, sitting on the couch while Mia showers and Ryan works out in her gym.

And all I can think about is how much I'd like to join her in that shower.

XOXO,

Tessa

February 28th, 1999 (10:30 am)

After dinner last night, Mia asked me if she could talk to me... alone. I was elated, but also nervous because I couldn't imagine where this was going.

That's an understatement.

"So, Tessa, I wanted to ask you a question," she began, sitting next to me on the couch. She tucked her legs under herself and leaned over toward me, taking one of my hands in hers, giving me goosebumps. "There is no pressure, and you can say no without any hard feelings."

Uh, okay? What on earth could she want to ask me?

"Do you have any interest in a threesome with me and Ryan?"

THAT IS SO NOT WHERE I THOUGHT THAT WAS GOING.

"I. Uhm." I said, stupidly.

"Look, I know you're bi because he told me. He and I have a history, as you know."

I just nodded, unable to find my voice.

"I'm sorry. I've made you uncomfortable," she said quietly after several moments. "I just, well, I may have been a little jealous last night."

"Oh, Mia, I am so sorry. I was trying not to be so loud, I swear. I know you and Ryan used to, well... you know. I didn't think there was anything more to it, or I'd never have done that, especially here in your house, and oh god, I'm so sorry." I blurted out.

"Tess, you misunderstand. I wasn't jealous of you because you were with Ryan. I was jealous of him because he was with you," she said softly, in that same husky voice from earlier.

"Me?" I mumbled. "You were jealous because you wanted to be with me?"

"Yes, you. You are cheeky and adorable and I wasn't kidding when I said you sound amazing when you come. I've been celibate for a while, my choice after my fiance cheated on me... but between the things Ryan told me about you, and talking to you, and then hearing you two last night, well..." her voice trailed off.

She was lightly touching my hair, and she had leaned her face close to mine. I stopped thinking. I just acted.

I took her face in my hands and just kissed her. Her lips tasted like the wine we'd been drinking, and it suddenly seemed a lot sweeter.

I have no idea where Ryan was during this. He'd let us be alone, and I honestly wasn't giving it a lot of thought at the time.

She kissed me back, eagerly. I felt like I was in a dream. I felt all floaty and lightheaded, and I don't think it had anything to do with the wine or the warmth of the fire. I was intoxicated by Mia.

Her hair was up in a messy bun, and I tugged it down. It's so long and thick and beautiful, and god, it smelled amazing. *She* smelled amazing, like vanilla and spice.

I pulled back, and I whispered, "you need to know something."

"What's that?"

"I've never uhm, done this."

"A threesome?"

"That, too," I replied. "I've never really gone much further than this with a woman," I confessed. "I've wanted to, but I've never had the chance."

Her dark eyes widened a bit.

"So," she said with a wicked look," you're telling me you're a virgin?"

"Well, I hadn't thought about it that way, but I guess in this regard, I am."

"Do you want to be?" She asked, as her hand cupped my breast.

"No," I replied, quickly. "Definitely not."

"Well, as hot as a threesome is, I don't think your first time needs an audience," she said, and she stood up and reached for my hand. "Come to bed with me."

"But... Ryan?"

"It's okay, Tess. He knew where I wanted this to go. He can entertain himself for now." I took her hand, and she led me to her bedroom.

God, it's hard to even find words to describe what happened between us. It was surreal. It was incredible.

I love sex with men, and this is especially true with Ryan, but this was so different. Just being touched by someone who understands your body the way only another woman can is incredibly erotic. She was so soft, so gentle.

Her body felt amazing. I couldn't get enough of her full breasts, her gently-rounded belly. I lavished her nipples with attention, determined to make her feel amazing, as amazing as she'd already made me feel.

Hearing her moan, hearing her whisper my name, god that was heady.

When I slipped my hand between her pliant thighs, she arched her back, pressing herself against it. I slid my finger inside her, my thumb rubbing her clit as I did. I felt her muscles clench down on my hand, felt her tremble in my arms as I kissed her while she came.

"Oh, Mia," I whispered against her lips.

She sucked my bottom lip into her mouth and bit gently down. I moaned loudly.

I came almost as soon as she touched me. It was everything I'd ever imagined it would be, but it had also surpassed my most vivid dreams, my hottest phone sex with another woman, and every fantasy I'd had.

She's about two inches shorter than I am, and with her being smaller than me, I felt so incredibly... protective maybe? I held her in my arms, and we fell asleep, naked, our legs intertwined.

When we woke up, I asked her if she was still interested in a threesome. Her lips formed a pouty smirk, and she nodded.

We went off to find Ryan, both of us naked. He was in the bedroom he and I had shared the night before, asleep.

We woke him up.

He wasn't sorry.

She told me she wanted to watch him fuck me. I swear I almost came again just hearing her say that. The two of them teased me and tormented me for what felt like hours. I can't remember how many times I came before Ryan finally slid inside me, and she kissed me passionately as he fucked me.

When I set out to be brave and bold, I had no idea this was where it was going to lead me. Last night was unbelievable. So was this morning when we had a bit of a repeat, except this time I wanted to watch Ryan fuck Mia. I laid beside them, my mouth wrapped around one of her nipples, my hand cupping and squeezing her other breast. When she came, I came... and no one was even touching me at the moment. Not even me. I'd never ex-perienced anything like that before... not just the obvious threesome aspect of it, but the kind of lust I've had for both of them, especially the passion I felt for her.

Now we're going to get ready for a hike on the prop-erty before it gets too late. It's supposed to snow, and I have every intention of kissing Mia in the snow.

XOXO,

Tessa

March

March 8th, 1999

Tonight, I went back to Fat Fighters. I was afraid I'd regained the weight I had lost, and then I also realized that if I missed another meeting, I'd have to rejoin. As it is, I had to pay for two meetings. They let you miss a few without paying, but then if you skip one, you have to pay, and if you miss three or more, you have to pay the membership fee again. Ugh.

I thought about just going, getting weighed, and leaving because I wasn't really feeling very social. I wish I had done that. Instead, I stayed and listened to women who look completely "normal" to me go on and on about how fat they are, how they can't lose the last five pounds of "baby weight," how they think their husbands/boyfriends find them less attractive because of it... etc, etc. It was miserable, and I spent most of the time wishing that the floor would just open and suck all of us into it so we had something else to focus on. How the fuck do I have a chance in the world of feeling normal or not ugly if these women who already have an ideal body can't even see it? I mean, seriously, three of the ones who were most vocal

57

are ALREADY AT A NORMAL BMI. They just want to be at the lower end of it, or they say they want to weigh what they did in high school because apparently people are supposed to be the same size their entire lives.

Good news is, if my goal is to weigh what I did in high school, it's not like I have that far to go...

ARGH.

More soon when I'm in a better mood.

XOXO,

Tessa

March 25th, 1999

Dear Book,

I am sorry for neglecting you, but I have a good reason. I've been spending a lot of time in NYC with Mia. She lives on the Upper East Side in this gorgeous building with a doorman. An actual doorman. It's crazy. Her apartment even has a view of the Empire State Building.

We go to museums, and we've been to the Central Park Zoo like three times already. We walk all over the city, holding hands and stopping to make out in the shadows of the buildings. I wasn't really sure at first what it would be like to be in public with another woman this way, but in NYC, no one seems to mind overly much. We've had a few snarky comments, but most people are just busy living their lives.

Mia introduced me to a folk-rock musician (Ani DiFranco), and I'm completely obsessed. We bought tickets to a poetry festival that is happening at Cooper Union next month, where Ani will be performing. I'm seriously psyched.

It's been really good between us. I'm not seeing Ryan anymore, but we're still friends. The truth is, I'm in love with Mia. I just didn't really want to be with anyone else physically, but I haven't told her. After everything that happened with Taylor, she's feeling pretty anti-relationship, and I get that, but I can't help it; I'm obsessed.

She tells me I'm beautiful and sexy. She makes me feel like I actually am those things. There is something very few people know about me, but when I was about 16, I made the idiotic mistake of shaving my face. I had some excess hair, and my then-boyfriend Jamie kept teasing me about it. He could be a real jerkoff. I finally got fed up and shaved.

Worst. Mistake. Ever.

Okay, maybe not ever, but it wasn't good. I know they claim shaving can't actually make your hair darker or thicker, but it makes it LOOK it at least... and I wound up with this permanent sort of shadow I can't seem to make go away. I hate it. It's something I am super self-conscious about, and I've never wanted any of the guys I dated to know.

That said, I've noticed guys avoid touching my face. I assume they feel the stubble, but I've never dared to ask because to be perfectly honest, the whole thing mortifies me. It probably shouldn't be a big deal, but it is to me. Once one of my father's brothers made a crack about it. He was drunk and showing off for a stupid girl he liked, and I was fucking furious (still am, honestly) that a grown-ass man would mock his 19-year-old niece for the favor of some twit who just happened to be a compulsive liar and half his age.

Anyway, I noticed something about Mia. She doesn't avoid touching my face. Even when I know she's able to feel it (like first thing in the morning). So I confessed what is one of my darkest secrets and told her. She said that she understands, particularly since she's half Italian and has her own facial hair woes (not to the same degree, but still).

It may seem silly, but this is just such a huge deal for me. I once thought I'd never be able to live with someone or get married (okay, a bit dramatic) because of this problem. I was so completely sure I'd never be able to tell a romantic partner. I can barely talk about it with even my closest friends, and I thought I'd be rejected for it.

I told Mia this, and I was crying because it was such a relief to get it out and to be accepted. She held me and she said, "Tessa, you are an amazing human being. I wish you could see yourself the way I see you. You're so hard on yourself about everything, and you're constantly doubting your self-worth, but you are lovely, inside and out, and I am so grateful I met you and get to spend time with you."

I wish I *could* see myself the way she does. She makes me seem pretty amazing.

She makes me *feel* amazing.

So yeah, I'm head-over-heels in love with her and every other corny cliche, and I have no idea what I'm going to do about it because I do not want to lose her.

I just don't want to fuck it up, ya know?

XOXO,
Tessa

April

April 1st, 1999

It's appropriate that it's April Fool's Day because I feel like the biggest fool right now. Mia and I broke up. Well, if you can even call it a breakup given that we were never officially a couple.

It's been going so well, and I've felt so good about everything. Then Taylor contacted her, and for a reason I cannot fathom, Mia agreed to talk to her. Taylor is supposedly truly remorseful for her actions and wants Mia back.

I was so upset, I cried hysterically. I said things I wish I hadn't. I basically told Mia she's stupid if she takes Taylor back, which was so wrong of me. She has a long history with Taylor. They were together for years, and they were each others' first loves. Taylor and Mia both come from fairly conservative backgrounds, and neither of their families was thrilled that they were together. Mia's mom mostly ignored it, but Taylor's family did what Scarlett's sister threatened to do and disowned her. So she gave up a lot to be with Mia in the first place.

Too bad she was also a fucking asshole who cheated on Mia and broke her heart.

The truth is, I love Mia so much, and I was both insanely jealous and truly terrified when she told me Taylor called her. I just can't believe that after all she put her through, Mia would consider taking her back, even for a second.

Part of me has to confess... I thought Mia was stronger than that. And smarter. And that sounds mean or petty or spiteful, but that isn't what I mean by it. It's just that Mia is so honest and open, and after being hurt that way by someone who lied to her repeatedly and cheated on her for months, it just doesn't *fit* with the Mia I know.

The Mia I know is confident, self-assured, secure. She told me she stopped dieting five years ago (she's 26 now) because she was sick of playing the game society told her she had to play. She inspired me to stop going to stupid Fat Fighters meetings by telling me that it was okay to just accept and love myself the way I am, that I'm worthy of that.

I am still not convinced it's true, but I'm trying. I want to believe it.

Yet, here she is, with someone who loves her, and she's considering going back to someone who betrayed her. And yes, I tearfully confessed that I loved her. I felt like a jerk for doing it when she was so confused and conflicted already, but I had to... I felt like she needed to know.

Then again, I also feel like she already knew.

It's one of the things about being with Mia. It's like she knows my thoughts before I even do. It's almost eerie at times, but it's also freeing because I feel like I can just be myself with her.

Now I've tainted it by being a bitch to her when she was struggling. I don't understand her reasons for even being willing to talk to Taylor, but she's certainly entitled to her feelings, and I can understand that she needs to sort it out.

Why couldn't I just have given her the space she needed? Why did I have to push?

Ugh.

We had a fight, a big one, and she asked me not to call her anymore. I'm heartbroken, but I also feel like I totally deserve it.

I went outside after the fight, and it was pouring rain. I just laid down on the deck and sobbed. I know it was a dramatic thing to do, but it felt cathartic.

It's funny. I've been in love before, or at least thought I was, but I've never felt this awful after a breakup. I've never felt so utterly devastated that I don't know how the hell I'll get out of bed tomorrow morning.

I'm seriously considering calling out sick from work tomorrow. It's Friday, and it would give me a long weekend to nurse my wounds and get my shit together.

I guess I'll see how I'm feeling when I wake up.

XOXO,

Tessa

April 7th, 1999

I need to talk about Easter. It was three days ago. So we usually go to my grandparents' for Easter dinner, and they have ham, scalloped potatoes, green beans... my mom is a vegetarian, so a lot of the time she makes this really good veggie casserole with swiss cheese, and sour cream, and those crispy fried onions. Dessert usually includes a coconut cake shaped like a lamb. Nothing says *Jesus has risen* like cutting into a cake version of the animal that represents him... or eating the actual animal, since sometimes they do lamb instead of ham for dinner.

And of course, there's always chocolate. My grandmother and I both love the Russell Stover chocolate coconut nests with the jelly beans. Someone will probably give me a white chocolate rabbit, since when I was a kid I preferred to eat only white chocolate.

And of course, all of it will be served with a heaping side of guilt about whether or not I really need a second helping of this or that, or whether I should be eating chocolate at all (the chocolate they fucking bought me), because that's how it goes.

This year, I decided I wasn't going to pig out on everything and blow my Fat Fighters regimen. I made a coconut mousse "pie" that had no crust and involved sugar-free pudding mixed with shredded coconut. I ate one piece of ham, a tiny spoonful of potatoes, and one roll with a tiny bit of butter. Then I passed on the chocolate and ate my mousse.

I spent all day feeling proud of myself. Afterwards, I went to the track by our house and walked three miles (I normally only do 1 - 1 ½) and came home feeling really great. That got kicked up a notch the next day at Fat Fighters when they asked how our Easters were, and I raised my hand and bragged about how I was totally "on plan" all day and had even done extra exercise. People clapped and told me how great it was. I had lost another 2 lbs (so current total is 35, but at least 5 of that is probably sadness over Mia since I'd stopped eating at all for a few days there).

I sat and listened to other women moan about how they ate everything in sight, and I have to admit that I felt pretty superior. I mean, if I could do it, surely they could've, too, right?

Except, I realized sitting there, as they talked about their families and the way they spent their day (aside from feeling like they'd been bad for eating too much food), I felt so disconnected from the holiday. I don't remember any of the family moments, and since holidays are generally the only time my family has moments I want to actually remember, that makes me sad. I was too focused on every bite I took and on trying to stretch out that one piece of ham through all of dinner. I felt hungry the entire time. I felt proud I was fighting that hunger, but now looking back, what was the cost? Would it have been so bad to just... eat? Just eat until I was full and then move on from that? I could've enjoyed the conversation and made some memories worth reliving in years to come. Instead, all I am going to remember is that this was the first holiday I was "on plan."

It even cost me memories with Olivia, because although she was sitting next to me, chattering away, I honestly can't remember a word she said the entire meal.

Suddenly, it doesn't seem like something to be proud of, after all. It doesn't feel worthy of celebration. It feels like a hollow, lonely, fake victory. Sure, I've lost more weight, but is it worth the cost?

I'm particularly concerned about the extra exercise I did that night. I didn't go "off plan," yet somehow it was like I still felt a need to punish my body for a holiday meal, even though I didn't even fully enjoy that meal. In fact, I skipped most of the foods on the table, including some of my faves (like my mom's casserole, which is so fucking delicious).

So why did I do that? Was it a control thing? Just to prove I could? I've also been forcing myself to drink WAY more water than I normally do. Like 90 - 120 oz a day, which has been fun at work where I need someone to cover me so I can go pee. I've come close to wetting my pants more than once... and I am sadly not exaggerating that. In fact, it got so bad one day last week that while I was waiting for Mike (the assistant director) to come cover for me, I had to stand with my legs crossed. I wasn't able to pick up one of the babies who had begun crying because if I had, I'd definitely have pissed myself.

All of this makes me think of Mia, and I think she's part of why I did this. Not because I think if I were thinner or prettier I'd get her back (though Taylor is both thinner and prettier than I am). No, it's because Mia rejects the idea of dieting entirely. She's embraced her curves. She eats what she wants, when she wants. She's a revolutionary.

She introduced me to the writings of a fat activist named Marilyn Wann and a book she found a couple of years ago called Intuitive Eating. Mia's belief is that she's happier and healthier now - as a non-dieter - than she was as a compulsive dieter who was still never thin enough (apparently even when she was actually thin). In fact, she believes dieting is why she isn't thin now. She started dieting in high school, and she was thin at the time (about 130 lbs at 5'5"). The dieting triggered nasty problems with intermittent binge eating, and she suddenly realized she'd gone from her lowest weight of 119 lbs to about 180 lbs in like eight months. That lead to another diet, and she'd gained even more weight up to her current 225 pounds. She told me that she'd realized she was done playing what she calls the *weight-loss game* and waiting for it to be her turn to win. She said it felt as futile as playing the lottery.

I think obsession with being "perfectly on plan" for Easter was about doing something I know Mia would discourage in her own gentle way. I mean, she told me I had to do what felt right for me and my body, so it's not that she'd push it, but I do know that the moral superiority I briefly felt in that Fat Fighters meeting is something that would piss her off, so I don't know... maybe that's part of what motivated it.

I wish all of this were easier. Everything is just kind of hazy right now. I'm going through the motions in so many ways, but I'm not really feeling all that connected to any of it. Not the dieting, weight loss, exercise... not the dating, not the heartbreak of losing Mia. I don't know what I'm doing. Work isn't even keeping me as happy as it usually does (possibly because I keep nearly wetting my pants).

XOXO,

Tessa

April 8th, 1999

I have decided to go to the poetry festival alone. I bought us the tickets, so I have them. They are "all-access" and get us (well, now just me) into all of the events, including Ani's concert.

I'm feeling pretty proud of myself for going to poetry readings and a concert in NYC all alone. I'm also feeling a bit terrified about it.

I bought a new top and a cute purse for the event. The purse is purple velvet with a drawstring, and it's embroidered with stars and moons, which I love.

I'm determined to keep my promise to myself about being brave, and this is just another step in that process. I have not spoken to Mia. I have no idea if she's back with Taylor. I guess Ryan heard we broke up, because he called me to tell me he was sorry. I thought about taking him to the concert, but I realized that it's something I need to do alone.

There's an open-mic poetry gathering, and I've even written a poem. If I'm feeling brave enough, I think I'll read it there, but I don't know. It's a bit scary to think about.

It's called "I Am Not," and it's all about how I'm not what society considers beautiful or "proper" for a woman, but I am still pretty awesome. Honestly, I am still shocked I wrote something that comes across so confident and strong, especially given that I have not been feeling either of those things of late.

I'll write it down below so that I have it saved in multiple places. Plus, it's a good reminder for me whenever I come back and read this entry again, which I'm sure I will. I do this every now and then. I go back and start reading from the beginning.

Sometimes I think, *good grief, was I dramatic much?* Or I laugh. Or I cry. Or I realize that I fall in love much too easily and suspect it's not really love at all. Except I ~~did~~ do love Mia. Right now, I kinda wish that one wasn't real.

XOXO,
Tessa

I Am Not

I am not pink satin trimmed in white lace
I do not fit into that pretty, baby-blue box,
with the tightly looped bow
I am not ethereal or lissome
I will never be Cinderella; my feet are simply not that dainty
My hair will rebel against its straight sisters
and lie in a tangled mess around my face
Like a reddish halo

I am a strong wine
Full bodied
Intoxicating
I will linger long after you drink in the last drops of me
My taste and presence
Imprinted indelibly on your lips...

~Tessa Elizabeth Alexander

Well, I did it! I went to the poetry festival alone. I also read my poem at the open-mic event. I was so nervous. They called me a "virgin" since it was my first time reading at one, which made me laugh and helped relax me a bit.

Afterwards, I was putting my poetry book back into my bag, and this girl came up to me to tell me how much she loved the poem.

"Tessa, right?" she started. I nodded. "That was really great! I loved it. How long have you been writing poems?"

"Oh, god... I have no clue. Maybe since I was in 7th grade or so?" I said. "So that would be uhm..." I hate math, especially when I'm nervous, even if it's simple math. In fact, sometimes I think the easier it is, the harder my brain freezes up. "I guess probably about 11 years," I finally said.

"I'd love to hear more of them," she replied. "I'm Sara."

I blushed a little. I was trying to figure out if she was flirting or just being friendly. I suck at that, by the way. It's even worse when it's another chick, because, I mean, I can't just assume every woman I meet who is friendly is gay or bi, and I'm still learning to read those signs. Hell, I'm still learning to read those signs even with guys.

Particularly since I always assume no one wants to flirt with a fat chick, and if they look like Sara, I think that all the more.

I'd guess she's about the same height as I am, maybe a smidge taller (I'm 5'6"). She's thin but with a fairly athletic build, like she's a dancer or something. Her long, blonde hair was tied in an enviable French braid (I can't do them to save my life) over her shoulder.

"Nice to meet you," I mumbled, a bit unsure of what to say next. I reached out and shook her hand. I felt a tingle run through my arm at her touch. She's not even my "type," so that took me a bit by surprise.

"Are you going to any of the other events?" she asked.

"Yeah, I have the all-access pass, so I'm going to the show tonight. I'm seriously stoked."

"Oh, wow! I'm so jealous. I tried to get tickets to see Ani's show, but they had sold out by the time I heard about it. Who are you going with?"

I felt kind of pathetic, given that the answer was, "no one."

"Well, I was supposed to be here with my girlfriend, but we broke up," I said after a pause. "So I decided to come alone. I have her extra ticket with me, and I'm happy to give it to you. I hate for it to go to waste."

"Oh my god! Are you serious?" Sara's blue eyes grew wide. "I'd love to. I mean, I can pay you for it," she said, grabbing her purse off the seat we were standing by.

"Oh, you don't have to do that!" I said. "I mean, it was just going to be wasted, after all. You're giving that empty seat a home."

"That's so sweet of you. At least let me buy you a cup of coffee," she replied.

"That sounds nice."

So we headed out of Cooper Union and went to a little diner nearby. We got a table near the window and started talking. She told me she's a grad student at NYU, pursuing her MFA in dance (ha! called it), but she's also studying psychology because she'd love to be a drama therapist eventually.

"I know I can't dance forever," she added. "Dancing really does a number on your body when you've done it for as long as I have."

I was impressed and also felt a bit ashamed (okay a lot ashamed) since I flunked out of Trenton State at 19 and haven't been in school since. It's a dream of mine to go back, but I have to pay off my old student loan first, and who knows when I'll get that done?

I normally avoid telling people about my horrible year at TSC, but Sara was so easy to talk to (which I'm sure will come in handy when she's a therapist). I found myself basically telling her my life story. I'm sure it doesn't help that when I'm nervous, I tend to babble and overshare.

"Wow," she said. "You've sure been through a lot. No wonder your poem conveyed so much strength and depth."

I blushed.

"Well," I began, "to be honest, I wasn't feeling my strongest when I wrote it. It was right after Mia and I broke up, and I was really struggling. Sometimes I read it to myself and think, *wow I can't believe this poem came from me.*"

She nodded. "I can understand that. I've seen videos of my dancing where I had that feeling."

"I always wanted to dance," I confessed. "When I was a little girl, my grandmother used to promise me ballet lessons, but first I had to lose weight. Then when I did lose weight, I still never got the lessons." I felt my face grow warm. I don't like to talk about my weight, really. Especially with a thin person. It just doesn't feel safe, and I always expect it to turn into dieting advice (because it usually does) from someone who has no idea what it's like to actually be fat.

"That's awful," she said, "and stupid. There's no good reason you couldn't have danced. Besides, if she was so hung up on your weight, why not have you take part in an activity like ballet since exercise can sometimes help? People can be ridiculous."

I found it interesting that she said that exercise can "sometimes" help with weight loss. I mean, hadn't my own experiences demonstrated that exercise is only so helpful? I was exercising like crazy and still barely losing weight for years. And man, I hate it, but hearing someone thin say that felt... validating. It should be enough

71

that my own experiences showed me that. I shouldn't need to hear it come from a thin person to believe it, right? Right.

Anyway, we spent about an hour there, and then I gave her the pass. I told her I was going to another reading event (not an open-mic one) and that she was welcome to join me if she wanted. Much to my surprise and delight, she accepted, and man, we lucked out, because Ani was a surprise guest reader and did some of her spoken word stuff! It was so cool.

After that, she had to go home for something, and she said she'd find me at Washington Irving HS later. The concert was general admission, so there were no assigned seats. Honestly, I didn't expect to see her again, but I'd had a good afternoon, so I didn't care.

However, she found me, just as she said she would. The show was amazing. Ani rocks. She's even better in person than on her albums (maybe this is why I so love all of the live bootlegs of her shows that I've picked up here and there). She has this energy that you just don't get as much of in a studio recording as you do live on stage. She's funny and sometimes seems a little awkward but in an adorable way.

But the best part of the concert was when Ani sang *Untouchable Face*, and Sara reached over and took my hand in hers. I was SO not expecting that development.

After the show, Sara asked me if I wanted to grab a drink. I don't have an ID, since I don't drive, but I've looked older than I am since I was 13. I was the one that my friends would use to buy cigarettes for them or rent the NC-17 movies at Blockbuster. She laughed when I warned her.

"It's Manhattan," she said. "They don't even card the kids who are obviously 17. You'll be fine."

And I was. I got a Long Island Iced Tea, because it was the only drink I could think of by name. I had no idea that it's also one of the most powerful drinks you can order.

It tasted amazing. I could barely taste the alcohol, which, apparently, the LIIT is well-known for, so when I had a second one, I was pretty much drunk. Despite being 23, I have never been drunk before (I know, I'm weird... blame it on being the child/grandchild of addicts), but I was thoroughly buzzed.

Thankfully, Sara figured out that I had no idea what I had gotten myself into and talked me out of ordering a third one, ha! She was drinking Corona, which I tasted and hated, but then I've never liked any beer I've tried.

After our drinks, she said that we should get a cab to Penn Station. "But you live down here," I protested.

"I know, but given that you're tipsy, I'll feel a lot better knowing you got off safely," she said.

And then... I leaned over and kissed her. I am so blaming the booze for that because it's not at ALL like me to make the first move (okay, maybe the hand-holding was the first move, but still). I was mortified, and pulled back, and began to profusely apologize, but she put a finger to my lips and just said, "shh..." and then leaned in and kissed me.

We made out in the back of the cab the rest of the way to Penn Station. She walked me down to the platform and kissed me before I got on the train. She passed me a piece of paper with her number and asked me if I'd like to do something next weekend.

So, I called her today, and we are going to a museum (which one is a surprise), followed by dinner and drinks.

I guess going alone worked out way better than I ever could've imagined, because I have a date with a smart, adorable, and quirky blonde next weekend. I'm feeling pretty awesome right now.

Or I was up until I tried to fall asleep and saw Mia's face behind my closed eyes.

XOXO,
Tessa

73

April 20th, 1999

I have to admit that part of me was worried that the date with Sara was too good to be true. She didn't seem like the type to play me, but it's happened before with guys. It's like some big joke to fuck with the fat chick's head and make her think you're into her... but Sara was not playing games. Or if she is, she's playing the long game, but I really don't think so. She's sweet and kind. We've had a lot of fun together. We went to the American Museum of Natural History on our first official date. It was great. She shares my love of gemstones, so we spent a lot of time in the Hall of Gems.

She held my hand as we walked through the museum, and I am still not used to people holding my hand in public. It's a clear signal to anyone watching that there's a romantic thing going on, and most of the guys I've dated have either avoided taking me anywhere public at all OR they've avoided touching me while in public when they did.

Though for all the shit Jamie (the first boyfriend) had put me through when we were dating on-and-off for all those years (from 13-19 for me), I will say he at least held my hand in public during our "on" phases. Still, he's one of maybe three guys who have in my entire life. Mia did, and that made her the first chick, but she was also the first one I'd ever dated. It was just nice to have that experience, to feel like I wasn't an embarrassment to this person who asked me out.

Sara and I also discovered something unexpected that we have in common. We were both put into psychiatric hospitals for eating disorders as teens. Hers was anorexia, brought on, in part, by her former dance instructor who had apparently been really obsessed with body size and told Sara she was too fat to dance the lead in a production. It led to Sara dieting secretly and losing about thirty pounds from her already-thin frame over about six months before her parents had caught on and sent her to an inpatient treatment center for it. She said she'd been under 90 pounds at her lowest weight, which is really scary, since she's 5'7" and has a dancer's muscle mass.

From what she said, this is part of why she doesn't believe in pushing people to change their bodies or putting pressure on someone to "look good." She was pushed that way, and while at first everyone told her how great she looked, she was literally dying. Her heart rate had gotten scary low, and she passed out a few times from low blood pressure. They thought at one point that her heart might fail. BUT STILL, she got compliments within the dance community (though her non-dancer friends began to express concern, and her parents eventually did, too). She couldn't even actually dance anymore by then because she was too weak.

Fortunately, they caught it fairly quickly. Everything I know about anorexia has taught me that this is a crucial factor in successful recovery. The longer it goes untreated, the harder it is to treat successfully. She's been in remission (her word for it) for five years now.

I talked to her about my issues with my weight and explained a lot of things I rarely talk about, including what had led to my hospitalization. Basically, I'd stopped going to school. I was 15, so too young to drop out, or my mom probably would've signed the papers just to avoid the fight. It all stemmed from the fact that she'd had her license revoked, so I had to take the bus to school. That was a problem because no one wanted me to sit by them, and we were far enough along the route that there were never totally empty seats available by the time it picked me up.

I handled bullies fairly well, mostly because I didn't give a flying fuck about their opinions, but the anxiety over the bus had been enough to make me stop going to school entirely, which got the child study team involved, and they ordered a psych eval. They determined I was suicidal and that my eating disorder needed inpatient care. I did NOT want to go to Pleasant Pines, but since I didn't have a choice, I am grateful it was one of the nicer (snooty, private) places. I had friends in some of the state-run facilities, and they were really awful. I think I only lucked out that way because those others didn't specialize in eating disorders.

Anyway, back to Sara. We haven't slept together yet. Well, we've slept together in the literal sense. I've spent the night, but we didn't have sex. We've had several really intense makeout sessions, but that's it. I am just not ready. Partly, it's my insecurities over my body. Despite the things she's said and the ways she's shown me she doesn't care, it's hard for me to trust that. Mia just had this magical way of putting me at ease, but it helped at least a little that while to ME she's not at all fat, I know that to society she is... Sara's totally not fat by anyone's standards (except maybe her former ballet teacher, but fuck her and her unhealthy, eating-disorder-promoting BS).

I explained to Sara that I'm feeling both conflicted about moving faster because of my still-unresolved feelings for Mia (I felt like I needed to be really clear with her on all of that because I don't want to lead her on), but also that I'm nervous about my body.

She was really sweet about both issues and said that she understands. She told me there's no reason to rush... she'd like to go further with this and see what happens, but she's also happy with where we are right now.

I was relieved and grateful for her understanding, and I can't lie; I am definitely really attracted to her. She has this seriously-adorable smattering of freckles across her nose. When she's happy, she crinkles her nose, and it's so cute. She's crazy smart, and I enjoy that. She challenges me intellectually but doesn't condescend. Her eyes are this gorgeous, crystalline blue. Seriously, they're so blue that they almost look supernatural sometimes, but they are the most intense thing about her. She's really easy-going, overall.

Between Mia and Sara, I decided I needed to come out to my mom, so last weekend, while she was doing some spring gardening, I told her.

"I'm not sure if Nate has told you, because he keeps threatening to, but well... I'm bisexual," I said. "I've been dating women recently, and I don't want to hide it. Plus, I'm tired of his threats."

My mom may have flaws, and we haven't always had an easy relationship (to say the very least), but to her credit, she just smiled and said, "Tessa, I love you and just want you to be happy. As long as the person treats you well, I don't care if you bring me home a son-in-law or a daughter-in-law."

I didn't imagine she'd have an issue with it, since she has multiple gay friends, but still, when it's your own kid, I think sometimes that can change things. So I was really grateful for her acceptance, especially after learning that Scarlet's family had threatened to disown her if she was with a woman. It was just nice to know that not all parents are like that.

XOXO,
Tessa

April 21st, 1999

Tonight was my first therapy session with Claire. As it turns out, she is familiar with the book Mia talked to me about, that one about intuitive eating? Well, the concept is that you re-learn how to trust yourself, and you eat what you actually like, stop when you're full, and don't obsess about calories, fat, etc.

It's simple, but because we've been taught not to trust our bodies from a young age, it's not easy. I am skeptical of the entire concept, if I'm honest. I mean, I've never had much luck recognizing my hunger before... I feel like I'm always hungry and like I am hungrier than the "normal" person. I am constantly craving foods, especially sweet foods. I don't think a sugar addiction is a real thing. The body requires sugar to stay alive, so are you gonna tell me that oxygen is also an addiction? I've seen REAL addictions, like heroin, coke, crack, booze... and I know what those are like, so I reject the idea of food as an addiction. All the same, can I trust myself to eat whatever I want, stop when I'm full (not stuffed and uncomfortable, but just right), and just let my weight do what it does?

I don't know. Giving up on the idea of being thin is tough. I've wanted it for so long. I've wanted a body shaped like Mia's, too, though, and I'd never have that, no matter what. Maybe the lesson there is to realize that what I think I want isn't necessarily attainable and that's okay?

It's overwhelming, but I like Claire, and dammit, I KNOW it shouldn't matter, but the fact that she's thin (like probably a size two) and telling me I don't have to be thin somehow carries more weight (no pun intended) in my twisted brain.

I will see her again in two weeks. Even with my insurance, I just can't afford weekly sessions on my salary. She told me to get the book, so I'm going to Barnes & Noble tomorrow after work to see if they have it. If not, I'll get them to order it for me.

In other news, I am seeing Sara again this weekend. I really enjoy her company. It's still surreal that she's into me. I'm just not used to the idea that anyone can like me for me without it being about liking my big boobs or something.

That's not how it is with Sara. We've been having fun

together. It's new, and I'm still really not over Mia, but Sara's a welcome distraction from that hurt.

Maybe that's a horrible way to put it. She's interesting, and smart, and talented, and I like her, but I cannot deny that her giving me something to do other than obsess about Mia is, well... I guess helpful?

At any rate, she's going to take me to a recital at NYU. She's not in this one, but I'd love to see her dance one of these days. I've seen videos, but I want to see it in person. She's going to introduce me to some of her friends. I'm really, really nervous about that. I know they're all fellow dancers, and that means they're almost certainly all thin. What will they think of Sara's date? I mean, she says they're cool with her being a lesbian, but a lesbian who dates a fat chick? Will they accept that?

Guess we'll find out, huh?

I'm hoping it goes smoothly. I'm nervous, but I think Sara's the type who'd stand up for herself, and what she wants, and who she's with, so hopefully, no one is rude to me (or behind my back later).

XOXO,
Tessa

April 26th, 1999

Sara's friends were all very cool. If they were shocked by my fatness or Sara being with me, they hid it admirably. If they said anything to her about it after, she opted not to share that with me.

We spent the entire weekend together. I enjoy spending time in her tiny studio apartment. It's really cozy, and it's in an area I really like, not far from Union Square. We watched movies, and listened to musical soundtracks, and she danced for me... a private dance that reminded me of a scene from Summer Sisters (except in the book, it's flamenco and not ballet). It was extremely sensual and erotic, and I couldn't resist taking things to the next level afterwards.

When you sleep with a woman, it's hard to say "we went all the way." It's not exactly as clear cut as hetero sex, is it? Not to me, anyway but I'd say we went all the way.

She finished her dance, and I pulled her to me and kissed her deeply. She leaned in, and tumbled on top of me (I was on the bed). I tugged her hair out of its messy bun and ran my fingers through it, tugging it ever so lightly. She moaned, and I nipped her neck.

A lot of it is kind of a heady blur. We'd had a couple of wine coolers, and I wasn't drunk, but I also wasn't sober. She smelled amazing. Her hair is so soft and long, and I am just obsessed with the freckles on her nose.

Anne Rice wrote in *Exit to Eden* that, "the next best thing to making a woman come is making her laugh," and I managed to do both... I kissed her nose, making her giggle. Then I slipped my hand between her legs and began massaging her through her leotard. I took her hand and placed it on my breast.

"Tess, are you sure?" she asked in a husky whisper. "I don't want to rush you - " I cut her off with a light kiss.

"I'm sure," I whispered back. "I want you, Sara."

Things got a bit... animalistic after that. We fucked and napped and fucked some more.

It was a perfect night.

Except... part of me couldn't stop thinking of Mia.

I feel so guilty for that. And pissed.

Sex with Sara was amazing. It was every bit as good as it had been with Mia. Maybe even better in some ways, but... I don't love her. The passion is there, but the emotions just aren't, and it's simply not as good without them, not for me.

I wish it wasn't like that. Sara and I have been very open, and I know she wasn't looking for anything serious when we met, and she knows I'm still getting over Mia (assuming you ever get over love that way).

But as much as I genuinely like Sara and enjoy her company, I don't think I will fall in love with her. I don't know. Does it matter? She knows where I stand. She knows what this isn't, so why can't I just enjoy what it IS???

Sigh.

It's just all so fucking complicated.

Ryan called me tonight, which isn't helping my current state of mind. He wanted to see how I was doing, and while we talked, he let it slip that Mia had not taken Taylor back. And by let it slip, I mean I asked him, and he hesitated but eventually told me.

"She said she can't ever trust her again, and she said she has you to thank for that clarity," he finally said. "Tessie, you should call her," he added, using a nickname I have always despised, yet when Ryan says it, somehow I find it endearing.

"Ry, she told me point-blank not to call her anymore, and I don't blame her. I was a jealous bitch, and I should've given her the time and space to work it out without acting that way. I was just so in love with her that I guess it clouded my judgment, but it doesn't make it okay. If she wants to talk to me, she knows how to find me. I'd answer. I just don't think she does."

He let it go after that, but now I can't stop thinking about it. Should I extend an olive branch of some sort? I have her email address. I could go to the library and use one of their computers since I don't have one. I actually don't have an email address, for that matter. I'm kind of terrified of computers. I blame Mr. Kazinsky, my 7th grade Computer Science teacher. He kept harping on how expensive each machine was (he said they were six grand each) and I freaked OUT. I refused to touch them. Then in 8th grade, when I had a computer class, I told the school nurse that computer screens gave me migraines in order to get out of it, but how hard can it be to sign up for an email address? I mean, I can Yahoo with the best of them.

I think.

Still, that doesn't answer the question of whether I should. I just don't know. I do owe her a massive apology. I should've trusted her to sort it out, to realize she didn't want to take back a cheating, lying POS.... and if nothing else, I didn't have to let my jealousy get the better of me and be a bitch about it.

I need to go to the library this coming weekend anyway; I have books to return. Maybe I'll consider it, and I'll at least get myself an email address while I'm there.

Maybe.

XOXO,

Tessa

May (be)

May 1st, 1999

I can't believe it's already May. This year is flying past. I mentioned that to my mom before she left for work, and she said to me, *that's what happens when you get old.* She's a wiseass. Besides, it's not like she's old, herself. She's only 40. Olivia had just giggled, but then she's not even eight, so to her, we're probably both old.

I'm babysitting Olivia tonight. She's probably my favorite person in this world and definitely the person I love most. I always wanted a sister. Nate is five years younger than I am, and we've always had a challenging relationship to say the least. I'd wanted him to be a girl (who I had planned to name Tinkerbell, naturally) and had been crushed when he wasn't. Since our parents split up when he was still a baby and our dad had gotten remarried, I never expected a sister.

Then, one night, when our mom was still using drugs, they ran into each other at a party. One thing led to another, and nine months later, Olivia arrived on the scene. They didn't get back together, and she was particularly horrified to have to tell us about the incident at all, though not as horrified as Nate and I were to hear about our parents' hooking up after being divorced for like tem years. We all adore Olivia, and I got the baby sister I'd always wanted, finally.

Except she's more like my daughter. When your mom's addicted to heroin, and your father's lost in bad life choices, and you happen to be about 16, you wind up being the parent. I was already the parent, even before Olivia. I was the parent to both of MY parents, which believe me, gets really fucking exhausting at times.

But Olivia... I just remember the first time I held her and she looked at me, and I felt like I needed to promise her I'd take care of her. So I did. I took her with me to live in Pennsylvania with our dad and his current (and third) wife Carly, who I cannot stand. She's a drunk, and a nasty one at that, but I didn't know it when we moved. Nate was already living there.

Anyway, my mom eventually got help and got sober. She's been clean for about four years now. She takes classes while Olivia is at school, and she works nights and weekends as a waitress. She's one of the hardest-working people I know. I admire the work she's put in to get her life back on track, even if I don't always agree with her choices. Sometimes it's hard because she's not really the warm and fuzzy sort, and I very much am.

I remind myself that my expecting her to be something she just isn't hardwired to be is on me, so I try to not let it bother me overly much. Emphasis on try.

I shower affection and love on Olivia instead so that she gets what I didn't.

Hopefully, it makes a difference later on in her life. I hope I can matter to her half as much as she matters to me. I was suicidal when I found out that my mom was pregnant. It was only a couple of months after I was discharged from Pleasant Pines. I'd been trying desperately to become a purging bulimic. I wanted to eat and vomit so I wouldn't gain weight. It's twisted, and I see that now, but at that time I couldn't. I was feeling like the biggest fucking failure. I couldn't stop binging. I couldn't make myself purge. I was unhappy with where we were living, and I'd just been through an ordeal that I haven't really wanted to admit had a big impact on me.

But I recently told Claire about it, so I guess it did have a big impact. There was this guy Josh that I'd had a huge crush on for years. This was the summer when my mom was pregnant with Olivia, and we'd been evicted from our apartment with nowhere to go. We were crashing on her friend's couch and floor. The deal was that I watched her three kids during her work day, and my mom was (in theory) out looking for a permanent place to live (she wasn't actually). Josh found out I was "living" not far from him and wanted to come over. I had told him no because of the kids. I didn't want us to get kicked out.

Josh ignored me and came over anyway. I was freaking out. It was a multi-family apartment building, and he'd somehow gotten into the lobby, and there were apartments right there. At least a few of the residents are elderly and home during the day, and he was being loud and obnoxious. The two younger kids were sleeping, and the older one was watching tv, so I told her I'd be back in a minute and went down to see what the hell Josh wanted.

Turns out, what he wanted was a blowjob. I had only done that a couple of times before and never to, uh, completion. I was like seriously pissed.

"Are you out of your mind?" I asked. "I have two little boys sleeping up there, and the girl is awake and watching TV. You cannot come up!"

His response? He pulled down his pants and swung his hard dick around like it was a helicopter rotor or something.

"Joshua, put your pants back on! Do you realize how much trouble you could get me in right now?"

He replied, "yeah, so suck my dick, and I'll leave."

85

I am still ashamed to say that I did. I felt trapped. For years, I blamed myself. I could've bitten him or screamed or just gone back upstairs and locked the door.

Every time I've remembered this incident over the years, I've felt dirty and gross, but Claire, in her calming therapist way, told me that Josh had been in a position of power and used it.

"He had the upper hand. You did what you thought you had to - not what you wanted to - in order to keep yourself, your mom, and your unborn sister from winding up on the street. You are the victim in this, Tessa. He's the dirty and gross one. He manipulated you and did not listen when you told him not to come over. He didn't listen when you said you didn't want to perform oral sex on him. **It's not your fault,**" she said fervently.

My dearest book, I've been waiting for a long damn time to hear someone tell me it wasn't my fault. I have always felt like it was. I wanted him to notice me for almost five years at that point. I wanted attention from a boy I thought was cute, but that wasn't anything like what I'd wanted, and I never saw or spoke to him again after that. I refused to talk to him when he tried to call.

What I've left out of the story is something that's so humiliating that it made the whole incident so much worse.

"You should feel lucky I even wanted a lardass like you to suck my dick," he said before he finally left.

I will never forget how utterly (and ironically) small and insignificant those words made me feel. It's how men have treated me so often over the years... as if I should count my lucky stars if they're interested at all, even if they're also too ashamed to tell their friends about me, even when I am not interested in them in return, but they pressure me, and I give in. It's like I should be kissing their feet in gratitude for their willingness to touch my fat body. I've even had more than one doctor who clearly didn't want to touch my body... DOCTORS for

86

fuck's sake. I mean, when a trained medical professional doesn't want to touch you and acts like your fat is contagious, it's pretty hard to feel good about yourself.

For years now, I have just wanted to be accepted and loved for who I am. I have literally never had that, or at least I hadn't until Mia. Not that she ever said she loved me, but she did make me feel loved.

It sucks. It hurts. I crave love, even more than I crave chocolate (and that's saying something because I really love chocolate). It feels like I'm not allowed to want or have either, simply because I don't have a "normal" size body.

Claire asked me what made me consider giving up on dieting.

I asked her if she was familiar with Sisyphus, and she nodded.

"Well," I said. "I felt like that. Like I keep pushing the same rock up a hill only to reach the top and have it roll back down. Then I have to start over. Except, unlike in the myth, I don't even keep reaching the top on subsequent attempts. In fact, I find the rock starts to roll sooner and sooner each time. For me, my rock is dieting and fighting against my body, and that hill is weight loss. Each time I diet, I lose less weight, even putting forth the same effort. Each time, it gets harder and harder, and I feel like... I'm broken. I feel like I'm standing at the bottom of that hill, staring at the rock and thinking *why the fuck do I keep doing the same thing expecting it to get better when it only gets worse and harder?*

She told me I have a way with metaphors, and I thanked her. She also told me that she understood why I'd see things this way.

I never needed validation in my life. I've always done my own thing, and approval was not something I sought out. In fact, I couldn't understand popularity or why anyone wanted it when it looked so exhausting and seemed to cost you your individuality.

Goddamn it if this particular bit of validation didn't feel pretty fucking awesome. It's like I think that as a fat person, I can't have these thoughts, which is illogical and absurd, but it's also what I've been taught everywhere I turn. Family, friends, the media... they all reinforce it.

Now I have to figure out how to untangle the nasty knot of emotions and conflicts it's created in my head. It feels as challenging as untangling Christmas lights and then searching for the dead bulbs.

I am determined to do it. I want to do it. I **need** to do it, because I am so tired of pushing that fucking rock up that fucking hill.

XOXO,

Tessa

May 25th, 1999

I know it's been a long time. I think this is the longest I've gone without writing here, but things have been very... interesting.

It started with me taking library books back (late, naturally, because god forbid I'm ever on time for anything - I swear it's genetic). I got myself a Yahoo email address and I emailed Mia.

This is what I said. I printed it out so I could paste it here for all posterity. I might've used a glue stick from work to do it.

```
Dear Mia,

I know you didn't want me to call you
anymore, and I want to respect that,
but I feel like I need to apologize
because it's been eating me up since
our fight. I wish I hadn't lapsed into
```

a temper tantrum of jealousy and said
those hurtful things. I know you needed
to figure out what to do about Taylor,
and I should've respected that this
was someone with whom you'd had a very
long, complicated history. I'm so sorry
for everything I said. I'm sorry for
not giving you the space you needed to
sort through it. I hope you have worked
things out and that however they turned
out, you are happier for it now. You
deserve that.

I meant it when I said that I was in
love with you. I was. I am still in
love with you. I have never felt for
anyone else what I feel for you. I'm
not expecting anything in return here.
I'm not even asking for a reply. I just
really needed to tell you this, to tell
you how truly sorry I am for any hurt I
caused you by not giving you the time
you so badly needed.

I ruined the best thing that I
have ever had when I destroyed the
relationship we'd begun to build with
my actions that day. I can't undo it,
and no amount of apologizing makes it
okay or acceptable, but I am sorry.

I want you to be happy, whether that's
with Taylor or someone else. You're
an incredible woman, Mia. You're
brilliant, charming, and beautiful. You
deserve someone who can see that, who
cherishes it, and who never takes you
for granted.

Well, that's all I wanted to say. I
am not expecting or asking for your
forgiveness, but at least you know I

really am sorry for my behavior.

Love,

Tessa

I didn't mention knowing she's not with Taylor, because I don't want her to be mad at Ryan (assuming he hasn't told her that he told me), and I really did not expect a response. And I didn't get one... at first, but I'll get back to that momentarily.

In the meantime, things with Sara were heating up. After having apologized to Mia by email, I felt a little more steady. I felt like maybe I was ready to let go of the past, of what I couldn't have.

As it turned out, Sara wound up wanting more from me than she'd planned when things started. She told me she was falling for me last weekend. I didn't see that coming, and I wasn't sure what to do with that information, either.

"I don't know what to say," I said. "I love spending time with you, Sara. I love making love with you. I love hanging out with your friends. But it's still new, too, and I threw myself heart first into my last relationship, as you know, and..." I paused.

"And you're not really over Mia yet," she said sadly. Her blue eyes filled up with tears, which made my heart ache. "I know all of that, Tess. I know you weren't looking for this, and neither was I. I knew telling you that I'm falling in love with you was a risk, but I had to be honest with you and with myself, because I *am* falling in love with you, and I'm scared of the feelings. I haven't felt this way about anyone in a long time, and well, it's exhilarating and exciting, but it's also absolutely fucking terrifying."

I took her hands in mine and kissed her lightly.

"I don't want to hurt you, Sara. I don't want to lead you on or make promises when I don't know what is going on in my heart right now," I finally said. I brushed a tear off her cheek.

"I know, and I love you all the more for it," she whispered. Then she kissed me. I pulled back because I didn't want to take advantage of her vulnerability.

"I don't know if that's the best idea," I said quietly.

She pulled me to her and kissed me again. "I just need to be with you, Tess. I need to show you how I feel right now."

And oh god, did she ever. She was so sweet, lavishing my body with kisses and tracing every inch of me with her delicate, graceful hands. I felt (as usual) self-conscious for a few minutes, since it was broad daylight (which I'd avoided with her as much as possible), but I quickly forgot to think about my insecurities as she worked her magic.

Why can't I just love her? She's wonderful. She makes me laugh. She is in love with me and *wants to be with me.*

I never thought anyone would love me, honestly. Not truly love me. I sometimes think Mia did, at least a little, but then again, if she had, would she have even had to consider taking Taylor back? Sara is here right now (well not literally right now, but you know what I mean), and she offered me everything I've ever wanted. Yet, I couldn't take it.

We ended our visit with her telling me again that she loved me and me telling her that we should maybe take some time apart while I sorted things out. She knew about my email to Mia, and I had told her how badly I wanted to move forward... how much I wanted it to be with her.

"But I just don't know if I'm ready, Sara. It really hasn't been that long, and this entire year has been a crazy roller coaster of intense, passionate relationships for me. I've never had anything like this before in my life, and I'm processing it all... probably badly."

Of course, being Sara, she was reassuring and sweet and told me that I wasn't handling anything badly, that she valued my willingness to be open and honest with her, and that my ability to communicate so freely was one of the reasons she fell for me.

So I went home. I spent the next few days talking about it with Vanessa, who thinks I'm crazy to still be hung up on Mia, even if she herself understands it since she's been in similar situations with guys she dated over the years. I talked about it during a session with Claire, who pointed out that I can't force myself to love someone and reminded me that this is the sort of behavior I've seen in my own father, behavior I've been careful not to repeat. I've always said I don't want to "settle" since I want something real, because I've seen the unhappiness wrought by settling.

But how can I think of Sara, of talented, sweet, wonderful, loving Sara, and think that it's "settling?" I asked Claire that, and she said that there's no real answer... except I don't love Sara, and I don't feel like that's going to change. For that reason, I'd be settling, and it would be deeply unfair to me and to Sara.

In that moment, I realized with stunning certainty that I was going to break Sara's heart, and the knowledge broke *my* heart a little. I didn't want to be *her* Mia.

So I talked to her, and I ended things. She cried but said she understood. She told me that her door is always open to me, whether I need a friend or a lover. I pointed out sadly that I hope for her sake the latter part is not true, but that I would love to remain her friend. I am giving her some space right now to heal and hopefully move on, but she's called me a couple of times. We have plans to meet up for a show in a few weeks. Or we did. Now I'm not sure. I don't know if Sara will want to stay friends in the end.

Because Mia called me. I just hung up with her after a four-and-a-half-hour-long conversation. She told me she didn't blame me for how upset I was and that she didn't feel a need to forgive me.

"Honestly, Tess, I've been wanting to call you since virtually right after the fight. Once I realized I couldn't ever take Taylor back, especially after being with you and everything that happened between us... but I also felt so foolish. I honestly wasn't sure you'd want to talk to me or see me again. Then I got your email, and I talked to Ryan, and he said I should call. I hope it's okay," she added.

Of course, I told her it was, that I was really happy to hear from her because I've missed her. A lot... and then, she said, "the thing is, Tessa, I'm utterly and completely in love with you. I was scared. When Taylor called me, it gave me the out I thought I wanted and needed, but I've been so unhappy ever since we stopped speaking."

I was speechless.

I've wanted so desperately to hear her say that. I want so badly to believe it, but her hesitation with me, her even *needing* to think about Taylor's proposition (regardless of her reasoning)... it hurt me deeply. Can I trust her with my heart? I just ended things with someone I knew wasn't going to hurt me, as much as we can ever know that, I guess, but I feel confident that I'd be safe with Sara, that she'd cherish me always, that she'd never stray. I don't know how I can be so sure, but I just feel it on a gut level.

Mia just enchants me. She's the night, and Sara is the day. It felt lovely to be bathed in the warmth of her rays, but I've always been a creature of the night, drawn to the stars and the moon instead of the sun. I want to be awash in Mia's moonlight, to wish on a star and have her be my dream come true.

I agreed to see Mia later this week in the city. I'm scared shitless, to be honest. It's what I've longed for, even when Sara was holding me, even when I was satiated sexually. My heart has craved Mia's love, and I think it's been this way for years, long before I even knew Mia.

It feels like she's the other part of me, the part that's been missing for my entire life.

If I don't take the chance and see what happens, I know I'll regret it forever. I guess it's time to be bold again.

Wish me luck. I think I'm going to need it.

XOXO,

Tessa

June

June 10th, 1999

Mia and I have spent the past two weekends together. Our "reunion" weekend, as I've been thinking of it now, happened to fall over Memorial Day, so we had all three days to talk and just spend time being with each other now that everything's out in the open and we're on the same page. I'm pretty sure we broke a record for the most times the words "I love you" have been used by two people in three days.

I'm deliriously happy; I'm fucking terrified. I'm not used to things working out, and I'm so afraid it's going to unravel, that I'll fuck it up, that she's not really in love with me but just wants to be, that she'll die (yeah, my brain went there)... etc. If it's bad, I've imagined it.

I'm going back tomorrow night, and as I have next week off for vacation, I am spending the entire week with her. She will be working three of the days I'm there, but I'll be at her apartment, waiting for her to come home. I'm going to try to make dinner. She has a gorgeous place, which she also inherited from her grandparents. It's got a huge kitchen (by NYC standards, anyway), and there's even a window over the sink. I want to do something romantic and sweet for her.

She gave me a key to her place last weekend and had the building manager add me to the list of people allowed in, so I no longer have to be buzzed up by the doorman when I get there. I feel so fancy and special.

We have even talked about me moving in with her. Not yet, of course, but maybe in six months or so if things keep going well. So of course, I'm panicking that they won't.

I'm fighting the anxiety. Claire has been so helpful. I am honestly so glad that I decided to go back into therapy, although she does think I need to see a psychiatrist. She pointed out that I've been coping with panic attacks since I was 15 without any medical help. I've been on antidepressants in the past, but my experiences weren't great. To be honest, I never felt like they did anything except make it impossible for me to shit.

Still, I am going to seriously consider it. If it might help me become healthier and better able to manage my fears and anxieties, it can only benefit my relationship with Mia, and really all of my relationships, I suppose. Even the ones with friends and family members.

Speaking of friendships, I could use some help in that regard. Van and I have been fighting a LOT. She said I'm never around, and I pointed out that we're together every day at work. It's not like she has a lot of free time on the weekends, anyway. Pete is pretty demanding of her time, even though they live together, and I know that part of what is causing the tension in our friendship is that they've been fighting a lot lately. Add to it that I've been over-the-moon happy and not really hiding it (why should I have to, really?), and yeah. I think it's just created a lot of stress and tension.

I want her to come to NYC next weekend to visit and meet Mia. Mia's totally onboard. She really wants to get to know my friends and even my family, since only my mom and sister even know about her at this point, though I'm not so sure about the family part.

It's not that I don't want to be open about it, because I do, but my grandparents are NOT going to be exactly warm and fuzzy about me being in a relationship with a woman. My dad probably won't care at all, but we don't really talk that often, and he's still living in Pennsylvania with his stupid wife, Carly. I definitely don't want to expose Mia to Carly.

Anyway, I really need to sleep. I've been staying up crazy late to talk to (and yeah, okay, have hot phone sex with) Mia every night, but she has an early morning tomorrow (like 5 am early), and I told her to go to bed.

XOXO,
Tessa

June 22nd, 1999

I'm not sure I've ever been happier in my life, and I am so fucking scared of it. I just expect something to go wrong, horribly wrong. My life doesn't work out this way. I never get to be happy for long. Something always goes awry. I know that sounds so moody and emo, and I probably sound like a broken record since I've said it before... yet I can't help it. It's true. It's just how it works, or always has.

With Mia... god, it's all so good. I may have accidentally mentioned to my grandmother that I have a girlfriend, and that was not so good, but I don't give a flying fuck. I'm happy. If she can't be happy for me, tough shit. The people who are supposed to love me most should be happy for me. If they can't be, I have no use for them in my life. Does that make me cold?

97

Mia's mother is not accepting of her daughter's sexuality. Oh, she's been fine when Mia's with a man. But whenever Mia dates a woman, it puts a rift in their relationship, which is really sad, since it's otherwise been such a good one over the years. Mia's father died when she was only 8. Her mom never remarried, because she said he was the love of her life, and she couldn't imagine spending her life with anyone else. On one hand, that makes me sad for her because she was very young to be a widow, but on the other hand, to have had that kind of love... that's impressive. That's rare.

Because her mom (Sharon) isn't open to her dating a woman, Mia hasn't been speaking to her much lately. She lives in Colorado, so it's easier to just avoid the subject. I am saddened by it, but I understand. Mia wants to meet my mom and Olivia, though. I told her Nate gets weird about same-sex couples, so I doubt he'll want to meet her. Frankly, he's been such a little shit since he moved back here from Pennsylvania (following a stint in juvie for harassment), that I don't want to subject her to him, anyway.

Tomorrow, I will ask my mom if she and Olivia want to join us for brunch at Mia's place next Saturday. I'm nervous as hell because I want it to go smoothly, but my mom is pretty sociable (I definitely did not inherit that trait), so I think it will.

Olivia can be shy, but I think she'll like Mia. She doesn't seem even remotely phased by the idea that her big sister has a girlfriend, but then again, she's not even 8, so maybe she doesn't quite get it.

I know this means telling my dad, since he'll hear it from Olivia, anyway, whenever they next talk, that is if Nate hasn't already told him. He's not going to like Mia because she has money, though. He's jealous of people with money. He'll assume she's a Republican (*as if* haha!), but he's not likely to meet her any time soon, anyway.

I'll try to write soon. I find it's harder to write when I'm happier. I'm using my happy energy on other things (yes, including lots of sex, phone or otherwise).

XOXO,
Tessa

June 30th, 1999

Well, I am sick. I have fucking bronchitis. Who gets bronchitis in the summer? Oh yeah. Me.

I feel absolutely miserable. I was going to spend this coming weekend with Mia in the city, but I can't sleep for more than a couple of hours at a time, and I don't want to get her sick. I am so disappointed about it because it's a holiday weekend, and we were going to go bar-hopping and have a picnic in Central Park. Mia has a friend who lives near the river, and you can see the fireworks from her apartment, so we planned to go there, too.

I couldn't even manage to get on the bus to visit her with how rotten I feel right now. She sent me flowers and told me to focus on getting better. She's so sweet.

Mom and Olivia loved her, and she loved them, too. Especially Olivia. After they left, she told me she really wants kids someday, with me. I was over the moon about that, since I would love nothing more than to be a mom eventually. And then...

Mia asked me to move in with her! Soon. As in September 1st, soon. Of course, I said yes! I'm moving in with Mia!!!

After that decision, we talked more about our future, about babies... about sperm donation or adoption. I am kind of afraid of adoption because you hear stories of people losing their kids when a birth parent wants them back, and while I understand the need to protect a birth mother's rights, it's just a scary prospect. I love the babies I work with so much that I know I'd love an adopted child like my own, and I'd be devastated to lose one that way. I'd also love to be pregnant or for Mia to be. She'd be utterly adorable pregnant. We've even started to talk about names a little here and there. I'd love to name my daughter in honor of Olivia, whose full name is Olivia Raven Elizabeth, so we were thinking maybe Ravenna for a girl or Oliver for a boy.

Okay, I think the cough meds are finally kicking in, so maybe I can sleep and dream of a future with Mia and our children.

XOXO,

Tessa

July

July 8th, 1999

Today, I was stupid. I had to go back to the doctor because, oh yeah, I AM STILL SICK. I now have pleurisy, apparently, in addition to bronchitis. The doctor was afraid I might have pneumonia, but I fortunately didn't.

That's not the part where I was stupid. That involved getting on the scale at the doctor's office. I've been refusing weigh-ins for a while now, per Claire's advice and with Mia's encouragement. I last went to a Fat Fighters meeting in April and hadn't been weighed since. At that point, I was 38 pounds lighter than at my first meeting.

Well, I've gained back 15 pounds.

I know Claire will tell me that this is not atypical. That early on, as you relearn how to trust your body, it's not at all uncommon to gain weight. That years of deprivation and restriction take a toll on our metabolisms. I know all of this, and I logically understand it, but emotionally? I'm freaked out. Really, totally freaked out.

I called Mia to tell her about the pleurisy, but I was ashamed to tell her about the scale situation. I'm ashamed both of the fact that I got weighed at all and of the weight gain itself, but she knows me too well. She immediately knew I was upset.

"Tess, what's wrong other than the pleurisy? I know there's something you're not telling me."

"Ugh, I'm embarrassed, Mia. I feel like such a fool."

"Sweetheart... c'mon. You know whatever it is, we can deal with it together," she said reassuringly.

So, through tears, I confessed my sins.

"Oh, baby," she said quietly. "You know it doesn't matter to me, right? I love you, not the number on the scale."

I sniffled. "I know," I said, "and I love you for that so much because I never thought anyone would feel that way about me. I want it to not matter to me, and I don't know why I can't let go and just shrug it off."

"Because who can, living in this world? Baby, I've been doing this a lot longer than you have, and even I have rough days. I know I don't face the same struggles you do because I am not as big, and I know my body shape is considered more 'ideal,' so I'm not minimizing what you deal with... not at all, but even with those benefits, if you will, I still have times when I momentarily think, fuck, I should be dieting, right? Or, I should want to be thin, right? It passes. You are bound to have moments like these, especially now when it's all so new and fresh. All I ask from you is that you promise to talk to Claire about it, and please sweetheart, don't shut me out or try to keep these things from me, not because you feel ashamed. You never need to feel that way with me," she added.

"Rationally, I know all of this. It's the emotional part I struggle with. I keep thinking this is all too good to be true, that you're too good to be true. The idea that anyone can just love me, all of me, unequivocally... it's a mindfuck, Mia. Everyone has always had some kind of, I don't know... expectations? In terms of what I should look like or weigh or do, and you just let me be me. The freedom is scary and liberating, and it's helping me figure out just what I want ME to be. I will always be grateful to you for that."

"I love you," she said simply.

"I love you, too."

"You need to try to sleep, okay? I'm worried about you. Go write all this in your book and then get some rest."

I laughed. "Sometimes you know me too well," I said.

We hung up, and now that I've written it all out, I feel a little bit better about it all. I'm not happy that I gained 15 pounds, but it is what it is. I've been active. I've been walking all over the city with Mia every weekend. I'm on my feet much of the day at work, picking up babies all the time, and I'm eating without too much stress or guilt for the first time in my life. My binges have significantly decreased, as has my stress eating. I'm learning how to cope with all of these feelings I've bottled up over the years.

Maybe I am 15 pounds heavier, but what I've gained in terms of sense of self is far more important, right? Right.

I will talk to Claire about it in our next session. I know it's too important not to, even if part of me wants to hide from it all. I know I need to understand it and try to figure out why it's so upsetting to me, beyond the obvious. It definitely goes deeper than the surface of "shit, I gained weight." It's got me doubting if I can trust myself, doubting if I can trust my body... doubting, well, everything.

Except Mia. Right now, at this moment, I have no doubts about her, which, of course, makes me have doubts about not having doubts.

On that confusing note, bed. At least soon I won't be going there alone every night. Soon, I'll be falling asleep next to her and waking up beside her every day. I can't wait.

XOXO,
Tessa

July 18th, 1999

Mia sent a car to get me from work on Friday. She didn't want me to take the train given how sick I've been. She's unbelievably sweet. She had another bring me home tonight, too, and since it was the first time we got to be together since she asked me to move in, it was extra-special. She gave me a magical blue box from Tiffany (not the kind with a ring, but maybe someday!). It had a keychain with a key to her apartment (even though I already have one), and it's engraved on the back with *9.1.99 ~ I love you, Mia.*

She told me that knowing how much I love that movie, my keychain just had to be from Tiffany, and that was so incredibly sweet, too. I get butterflies every time I look at it.

I am finally feeling better, and oh god, I had missed her so fucking much. Talking on the phone is wonderful, and we can spend hours doing it, but it's not the same as being able to touch her and hold her and just SEE her when we talk. We spend a lot of time playing board games or silly little games we make up. She kicks my ass at *Monopoly*, but I usually beat her at *Scrabble*.

This weekend, we went to see *The Blair Witch Project*. It was SO fucking good. OH MY GOD. It was scary as hell, but in a way I've never experienced with any other movie. I absolutely loved it. They've been doing these brilliant ads for it that make it seem like it's "real," and I totally dig it.

We did have an unfortunate incident during the movie, or really right before it. She and I had been sitting and holding hands, and some bitches behind us started making snarky comments about the fat lesbians. I fumed, particularly since one of them was probably the SAME

SIZE AS MIA... so who the fuck was she to say that?

Mia just squeezed my hand and whispered, "Babe... remember that fat isn't a bad word unless we let them make it one." Then I felt calm(er).

After the movie, it was our turn to laugh when we heard them talking about how they really hoped that someone eventually found the lost filmmakers! They apparently believed it was a documentary, hah! Sooo, they weren't just bitches, they were stupid bitches. My favorite kind.

I wish I could say I was totally unfazed by the entire incident, but it rattled me a little. Being called fat isn't new. Being called a fat lesbian is. I'm not ashamed to be in a relationship with a woman, but the idea that people feel a need to mock our sexuality that way is a bit distressing. Mia's had more experience with this sort of thing than I have, especially since she initially came out as bi back in Colorado, and they were less accepting where she grew up than here in NYC.

We definitely benefit from being here, in a city that's far more gay-friendly than many places. I can't imagine how hard it must be to be gay (or to "appear" gay, since neither of us is actually gay) in like Iowa or something. It makes me sad. I can't understand how anyone can view same-sex love as some kind of "threat." For fuck's sake, both of my parents are straight and have been married and divorced. My dad's been married three times, for crying out loud. How is HE not violating the sanctity of marriage or some such shit? Sigh.

The rest of our weekend was amazing. The only part that made me sad was that it was too damn short. I really wanted to spend more time with her, but having been out sick for over a week, I couldn't stay. Trista, the new director (who I can't stand) would probably fire me if I call out tomorrow.

So, I'm home, but I've been very thoroughly loved this weekend, in all respects (dirty and not dirty). I feel such peace, and I haven't been this relaxed or happy in a very long time.

XOXO,
Tessa

July 24th, 1999

Oh my god, I ran into KEVIN of all people today. I was at the library here in Cranford, and he was using the computer next to mine. I didn't even recognize him at first. I was focused on what I was doing and suddenly heard someone say my name. I turned, and my jaw dropped.

The first thing I did was glance at his left hand and notice he wasn't wearing his ring. I wondered if that meant things were over with Kelly. I decided I wasn't asking.

"How've you been?" he asked.

"Busy, but good. You?"

"It's been a bit of a roller coaster, but I think it's getting there," he replied, somewhat cryptically. "Listen, can I take you for a cup of coffee? I'd really love to catch up."

I hesitated, but I was curious.

"Yeah, sure. Let me finish this email, and then I am free."

We went and got coffee. My hunch was right. He left Kelly not long after our "date." He said he tried to get her into couple's counseling, but she refused, and at that point, he felt like he had no alternative. He even confessed he'd thought about cheating, which in my opinion is a little bit of an understatement. He'd absolutely have cheated if I'd been a willing participant that day, but anyway...

"I have to thank you, Tessa," he said. "I'm not happy things happened this way, and I'm not proud of the fact that I went out with you and was, well..."

"Willing to cheat with me?" I supplied helpfully.

"Yeah," he said with a bit of a frown, but I wasn't sorry I'd been so blunt about it. "Look, I didn't leave Kelly because of you, even though I admit that our conversation that day gave me a much-needed push to face the problems in my marriage. I never called you again, because I couldn't imagine you'd want to see me, but I've thought of you a lot, and well... is there any chance we could go on a real date some time?"

I've gone most of my life feeling invisible, which is strange when you're so big and made so very much aware of it, but this year has been crazy. First with Kevin, then Ryan, then Mia, and finally Sara. Now, of course, I'm really with Mia... and now Kevin's asked me out again? It's crazy. My brain is feeling like someone's playing a practical joke, like there must be hidden cameras where they laugh at the fat, bi chick who thinks people actually like her and actually want to be with her.

"I am sorry," I told him, "but no."

"You have a boyfriend," he said. "I should've known."

"Actually, no. I have a girlfriend," I clarified, "but she is amazing, and I've never been happier, so I won't be dating anyone but her, hopefully for the rest of our lives. I'm moving to NYC to live with her in September."

"Wow," he said. "Well, I'm happy for you. You're a great person, Tess. You deserve it."

"Thanks," I said. "You will find the right person eventually. Just don't settle. If I've learned anything over the past couple of years it's that it's worth waiting for it to be right."

He offered to drive me home, but it wasn't far, so I just walked.

I came home and called Mia to give her the scoop. She just laughed and told me she couldn't blame him one bit for wanting a second chance with me. God, I love her.

XOXO,

Tessa

July 25th, 1999

It's 1 am, but Mia just called me in tears. Her mother's dying. Brain tumor. They don't know how long she has, but it's inoperable and hasn't responded to treatment. Mia's devastated and angry because her mother didn't even tell her she had been sick to begin with, and I can't blame her for that. I'd be angry, too. I know things have been strained between them because Mia's with a woman, and her mom doesn't approve, but how can you not tell your only child you have cancer?

Here's the part that has me freaked out. She's asked Mia to come to Colorado. She can't be alone anymore, and she said she wants to try to make peace before her death.

Mia hasn't said no.

I get it. I'm trying so hard not to be selfish in this. It's not about me, and I know that, yet part of me is terrified that this is the end for me and Mia.

I can't imagine my life without her in it. How will I cope if this is what ends us?

How can I think of myself when Mia's hurting and faced with her mom's death? She already lost her father so long ago. Now she's going to be an orphan, and while she may be over 18, that doesn't mean it won't suck or hurt to be parentless. I don't even have the best relationship with my own parents much of the time, and I can't imagine either of them not being in my life.

Oh, dear Book... I want to be with Mia. Like I told Kevin, I want to be with her for the rest of my life. I can't imagine losing her.

So what if I do?

XOXO,

Tessa

108

August

August 1st, 1999

Today, I saw Mia off at the airport. I am gutted. She's gone. I'm not moving in with her in a month.

She has left behind her life here in the east, including me, to go care for her mom. I wanted to be sympathetic and understanding, and on the surface I was, but saying goodbye to her was the worst thing I've ever experienced.

As we parted ways at the gate, she cupped my face in her hands.

"Tessie," she whispered, which was odd because she rarely calls me that. "I love you so fucking much. Please know I've never loved anyone else this much."

I stifled a sob. She leaned in to kiss me, her long, dark hair falling like the night around our faces. Tears filled my eyes. This wasn't happening. How could this be happening?

How can two people who love each other this much not be able to make things work somehow? It isn't fair.

"I'll miss you," I whispered against her lips. *Take me with you*, I pleaded silently.

She made her choice. She chose her mom. Her mom

who won't accept that her daughter is in a same-sex relationship. I can't go with her.

I don't know how I feel, exactly. Angry at Sharon for not wanting her incredible daughter to have love, especially when she herself knows how fragile and rare it is, given that she lost the love of her life so young. I'm hurt by Mia's actions and angry with her for choosing a mom who won't truly accept her, because of our relationship. Crushed at losing her. Angry at myself for not being more sympathetic to Mia's plight.

I haven't said it. I don't want to hurt her even more. I know this was not easy for her. I believe she loves me, but still, part of me thinks *if she loved me enough, would she be leaving?* Why not take me? I have nothing keeping me here, except Olivia, of course, but we'd visit. I'd email her and call her. It would be hard, but it would be worth it to be with Mia.

I keep thinking I could never be so selfless in Mia's position. To care for a dying parent, at the cost of my relationship, when that parent didn't give a shit about my happiness?

I wanted to try long distance. I told her I'd wait for her... which I suppose is waiting for her mother to die, and that made me feel guilty, but Mia insisted she didn't want me to put my life on hold indefinitely. Her mother's doctors say she could have six months to over a year. It's terminal, but it's a slow cancer. It's affecting her memory, her motor skills, everything, so she can't be alone, and Mia didn't want her to go to a home.

For Mia's own sake, I understand why she went. She is who she is, and it's why I love her, even if I can't quite comprehend that kind of devotion to a parent who wants to deny you in that way, but the guilt of not doing this would've consumed her. So, I don't begrudge her making this choice, and I know it was what was best for her.

But why did it have to mean our end? Why did we have to break up?

She told me it was because she loved me too much to keep me from moving forward, but I wanted to move forward with her, not alone. I was about to move in with her. I was going to go back to school in January.

Things were moving forward. Now, everything is... over.

And I am broken. I am lost.

XOXO,

Tessa

August 4th, 1999

I haven't worked all week. I didn't have any sick days left, but I called out anyway. It's a fool's move, but I just couldn't do it. I can't be responsible for taking care of babies when I can't even take care of myself right now.

Mia called last night. She wanted me to know she's gotten settled, has seen her mom's doctors, and is renting out her apartment in Manhattan. She offered it to me, rent free, so I could go back to school, but I couldn't accept. Not only because it's too much, but because I can't bear to be there without her.

As for school, it will have to wait. I can't do it while I work at this job. I love my job, but I know my limits, and it's just too much.

I saw Claire today. I didn't want to go. I've cried so much in the past few days, it feels like more than I've cried my entire life up until now. I tried not to cry with Mia on the phone last night, but I lost that battle.

It was okay, since she lost it, too.

"I already miss you so much," she whispered through her tears. "I'm so sorry, Tessa. This isn't what I wanted for us."

"I know," I answered. "I'm sorry, too." We hung up.

Today, Claire asked me how I felt about everything in that way therapists do, and I basically lost it. I confessed how angry and betrayed part of me feels, how I feel like everyone always abandons me, and how I feel such tremendous guilt for thinking that way when Mia's dealing with her mom's illness, and when I know she's also hurt over this.

"But it was her choice," Claire interjected. "Of course, not her mother's illness, but to end her relationship with you. You'd have gone with her. Did she know that?"

I nodded. "Yes. She knew."

"Then while I can understand her logic, and I imagine you, with your analytical mind, also can, it is entirely understandable that you'd feel so hurt and betrayed. But here's the real question you need to ask yourself. Are you going to keep talking to her? Because I don't see how that is going to help either of you with moving forward."

I know Claire is right. I agree with her. I can't move forward as long as I am talking to Mia. But am I strong enough to cut her out of my life completely? Even if it's what's best for me?

XOXO,
Tessa

August 6th, 1999

Mia just called again, and things didn't go so great. We were talking for about fifteen minutes, but Claire's voice was in my head the entire time. I knew I was going to broach the issue, and I was dreading it.

"I love you."

"I know that," I replied. I'm not sure why I didn't say

it back. It's certainly not because I don't love her, but I think I was just feeling so hurt that I couldn't do it. It was undoubtedly passive aggressive in part, and I hate that, but it also made me realize all the more that Claire was right. I don't want to destroy the memories of what Mia and I have shared by lashing out or being a bitch... and my defenses were up. Which, of course, Mia sensed.

"Are you okay?" she asked after a moment of silence.

"Mia, you just moved most of the way across the country. I thought I was moving in with you in a few weeks. My heart is broken into a million pieces. No, I'm not okay. I'm trying really hard to be understanding and patient and supportive, but I'm really struggling here. I am crushed. Right now it doesn't feel like I'll ever be okay again. And I feel so selfish for thinking of me when you're faced with your mom dying," I added.

"Tess," she whispered. "I'm sorry. It was a stupid, automatic question. I'm not okay, either."

"I know, but Mia... I love you, and I didn't want this to be how it worked out, but this is where we are now. You made your choice, and I respect that, but if we're over, if I'm truly supposed to be trying to move on and not keep my life on hold..." I paused as my voice broke and a new flood of tears spilled down my cheeks.

"Mia, you have to let me go. You can't hold on part of the way. I can't talk to you, at least not right now. Maybe down the road, someday, somehow we could be friends, but if I'm honest, I doubt it. I can't do halfway. I am either with you, or I'm not, and you have to respect this. This is what I need. Please believe me when I say that it is not at all what I want."

"Tess... I don't know how to let you go. I love you so much. I'm so sorry I've hurt you."

"Look, Mia, I know. I know this wasn't your choice, at least in as much as I know you don't want your mom to be sick and you don't want to lose her. I don't want that for you, either, and I'm sorry that this is how it is, but the choice to go to her, to take care of her for however long she has left, that was your choice... and one you intentionally left me out of. I'd have come with you, Mia, and you knew it. You didn't want me to, and while I understand that it would've complicated things with your mom, I can't pretend that it didn't hurt like hell. I love you so goddamn much, Mia... but you're the one who said, who insisted, that we were over once you left. You can't keep me hanging on by a thread this way. I want to be supportive, and I wish I could be there for you, but you didn't want that, and I can't change that. Now, I have to protect myself. Now I have to put myself first. It kills me, Mia, but talking to you like this, it hurts. I can't do this over and over indefinitely," I sobbed. "I'm sorry. I have to go. Please don't call me again. If you truly love me, and I believe you do, you have to let me go now."

She just whispered, "Okay, Tess. I love you."

Then she hung up.

I have never felt more alone in my life.

And oddly, as much as it hurts, as horrible as it all is, I've also never felt stronger.

XOXO,

Tessa

September

September 8th, 1999

I know it's been over a month. I just haven't been up to writing. Well, that's not true. I've been writing a lot of poetry, pouring out my emotions through words that way, because it's just been easier. Besides, here I'd feel like a broken record. I love Mia, I miss Mia, I can't believe she left me...

She's left me alone and hasn't called. I have talked to Ryan and asked how she is because, well... I am still in love with her and can't help it. He said she's as well as can be expected, that she's been spending time with her mom and volunteering at an animal shelter part-time. He also said she is miserable without me, and I couldn't help but point out that that was her choice. He didn't disagree and actually told me that he thinks she made the wrong decision... that if he ever found what he saw she and I had, he'd never let it go the way she did. That validated my feelings a bit, and I hated that I needed that validation, but while Claire has, of course, helped me better understand things, she's also not friends with both of us. She's my therapist, and I'm her client, and she's not there to "take sides" this way.

Ryan and I are going to a movie this weekend. He's trying to distract me, and he said I need to get out. I know he's not wrong, and I don't have to hide my sadness from him, so I'm trying to look forward to it.

XOXO,
Tessa

September 12, 1999

Oh, god. I slept with Ryan last night.

I don't know how I feel about it. I mean, I know how I felt *during* it, which is to say fucking phenomenal, but part of me feels like I betrayed Mia, which is stupid because she broke up with me over a month ago. She ended it, not me.

I mean, it's Ryan. She'd probably be happy that when I did finally move on, even just for sex, it was with him. After all, we've both *been there, done that* with him. Hell, we even did *that* with him together the weekend she and I met, right?

To Ryan's credit, I initiated it. I'd had a glass of wine and was a little buzzed. He tried to resist, saying I was drunk and emotional.

"I had one glass, Ry... even I'm not that much of a lightweight. I just want to feel something other than sad. I need to escape, and you can give me that."

I leaned in and kissed him, and he kissed me back, rather passionately I might add, but then he pulled away again.

"Tess, I don't know. This seems like such a bad idea. You're vulnerable, and I don't want to take advantage."

"You're not, Ryan. I started this. I want this. Hell, I need it, but not if it makes you uncomfortable or if you don't want it..." I stood up, taking my empty glass to the kitchen. He followed.

"I can just go home," I said quietly.

"Fuck it," he said, and he pulled me to him. "You're sure?"

"Are you?" I countered.

"No, but oh, god I want you. I have all day."

"Really," I whispered, my lips against his neck. "Show me."

And, oh god, did he. Multiple times. Including right there in the kitchen. He bit my neck; he pulled my hair. He made me come three times before he fucked me up against the kitchen wall.

Then we made our way to the bedroom. By the time I left tonight, we'd had sex five times, and I lost track of how many orgasms I'd had.

My body feels thoroughly used and exhausted, and I needed it. I wasn't wrong about that. I also needed it with someone who understands my situation and knows my emotional state right now... with someone who was prepared to make damn sure I knew what I was doing when I started it all.

I don't know if he'll tell Mia. Since they're still friends, he may feel obligated to, and I understand that. I don't care. She wanted me to be free, right? Well, this was me being free.

So why do I feel so awful and guilty?

XOXO,

Tessa

Well, I didn't feel so awful and guilty that it kept me from repeating the performance. Several times. Ryan and I have spent multiple nights together. I'd forgotten how incredible he is in bed. And in the shower. Against kitchen walls. On the floor of the living room. Bent over the side of the couch. You get the idea.

We did talk about Mia and whether or not he's going to tell her. He said he had wanted to talk to me about it before saying anything, because he didn't want to betray my trust. I told him he's still friends with her and that it would feel dishonest to me not to tell her it had happened. He agreed but said he's not going to volunteer it unless she asks about me and how I am, which I guess she does with some regularity.

I wonder how she'll take it. So does he.

In other news, I had a very unexpected call... from SARA.

I haven't talked to her in months. We saw each other a couple of times after Mia and I got back together, but I think it was hard for her. I know Mia was a little jealous, not that she had any reason to worry.

She asked me how I am, and then she asked about Mia, so of course, I began crying, which made me feel like such an asshole because A) I've been sleeping with Ryan and B) Sara was in love with me. Then again, she did ask, and she knew I was with Mia, so I guess it's okay.

Anyway, she told me she was sorry, and I know she means it. One of the things I can say without doubt about Sara is that she's incredibly genuine. She doesn't say things she doesn't mean, which is one of the things I always really liked about her.

She asked me if I wanted to meet up. I hesitated, both because I don't know if it's leading her on and because, frankly, part of me wants to keep my time open for more steamy sex with Ryan. Claire and I talked about Ryan, and she's concerned I'm using sex to avoid dealing with my feelings, which is valid and probably true to some degree. I pointed out to her that I'm just naturally a very sexual person, and it's been hard to be alone after having someone steady for what was (for me) a fairly long period of time. It's not like I'm hooking up with random strangers or being careless, either. I'm on the Pill, and Ryan and I are being careful.

I really do like Sara, even if I wasn't in love with her, and I could use another friend. Vanessa and I have spent very little time together, lately. She quit her position at the daycare and has been busy with Pete the douche and her new job. Plus, there's just been this weird rift between us, and I'm not really sure why, but I am tired of chasing her down to try to figure it out, so I've decided to give her the space she apparently needs to figure out what she wants from our friendship.

However, this has left me kind of friendless, aside from Ryan. While he's a great guy, he's still... a guy.

I finally agreed to see Sara next Saturday. We're going to go to see her friend's band perform at The Bitter End, which is good, because it's somewhere I never went with Mia.

I'm still nervous about it, but she said a few of her other friends are going, so it's a group thing. That makes me feel a bit less on edge.

I'm supposed to live my life, right? Isn't that what Mia wanted me to do?

Too bad it still kinda feels like I'm just biding my time, waiting for her to come to her senses.

XOXO,

Tessa

September 30th, 1999

Things with Sara have gone smoothly. I think we've successfully made the transition from exes (if we really were that in the first place) to "just friends." She's dating someone new, as it turns out. Her name is Sasha, and she's an international student from Ukraine, which is cool to me because my great-grandparents were from there. Like Sara, she's also a dancer. She seems really sweet, and I like her a lot. Sara seems happy with her; that helped me ease into things a bit more.

Ryan finally told Mia about us, and he said she cried. Which made me cry, even though part of me felt like, *What did she expect? That I'd stay celibate for the rest of my life?* He said she wasn't mad at him (or me, not that she'd have any real right to be).

We've been meeting up once or twice a week for dinner (and yes, hot sex), and he drops me at work the next day (if it's not a weekend). I honestly had forgotten how much we have in common and how well we get along. It's not just lust, even if I'm not in love with him by any means. There's genuine affection and care, and that's nice, especially when I'm feeling so raw.

I was telling Claire that being with Ryan is good for my self-esteem. He makes me feel fantastically sexy in a way that no other man ever has. Since Mia left, I've been struggling more with my food choices. I've binged a few times, and while I logically understand why that has happened, it's been hard to process it without resorting to my old eating disorder / dieting behaviors where I follow a binge with an extreme phase of food restriction. That inevitably leads to another binge and more guilt, and while I've been walking at the nearby running track regularly, I've been enjoying it just because it feels good and not because I'm hoping it makes me skinny. I like it because it's mindless... I put on my Discman and zone out.

I'm really trying. I don't want to lose the traction I gained this year in terms of accepting myself as I am right now. I spent so much of my life waiting to do things because of my weight, because I thought I was too fat to do them... and if I hadn't met Ryan and Mia, I'd probably have stayed on that path and lost even more of my life to a pattern that was never going to have the fantasy happy ending I wanted it to have.

I know now that I can be fat and be worthy of love and that I can find love. Mia gave me that gift, and frankly, so did Sara. In some ways, Sara even more so, because with Mia, well... she's a radical. She's anti-dieting; she's all about fat acceptance and promoting the idea that you don't have to be thin to be happy. There was no way in hell I could've imagined that someone who meets societal conventions of beauty would ever want me and not feel the need to hide it, since most of the guys I met wouldn't have been caught dead with me in public. They just wanted to fuck me.

Sara didn't just want to fuck me. She fell in love with me. She introduced me to her friends. She truly accepted me as I am. She met me in person first (not on the phone) and wanted me anyway.

I've been telling myself not to "settle" for over a year and a half, but this year is the first time I really believed that I didn't have to settle if I wanted a friend, a partner, and a lover. Someone who could give me everything I deserve and then some.

Yeah, I know it shouldn't matter that Sara's thin and wanted me, or that Mia is gorgeous and could be a model but wanted me, but I can't help it. It sometimes still doesn't feel real that **anyone** would want me. My own family doesn't seem to even care for me most of the time since they wanted me to be something I'm not (thin).

When I shared this with Claire, she helpfully reminded me that healing is a process, and that I'll get there. I am starting to think she might be right.

So yeah, maybe I'm roughly the same weight I was at the start of this year. Maybe my "pact" with myself that I made last December to either "do something about my weight or accept being fat forever" hasn't exactly gone the way I expected it to at the time I wrote that. Instead of dieting, I am learning to love the person I am now, not the person I think I should be. That feels so much better than I could've imagined. Although, who am I kidding? I never would've believed accepting myself "as is" was an option.

Even though Mia broke my heart, and even though I am still in love with her, she also gave me quite a gift. I can't hate her. I can't even be angry with her anymore. I was at first, but it's not fair to be angry at her for doing what she felt she had to do in an impossible situation. I can't say I'm not still hurt, because that would be a lie, but I'm trying to work through it, both in sessions with Claire and with the help of friends (though not Van, to my sorrow).

Speaking of which, I made plans with Vanessa. I want to talk to her to try to figure out what's going on and why she's been so distant with me. We have never been great at communication, which is odd since we've been friends for so long, but maybe it's because of that in some ways. I mean, we weren't even in school yet when we met. So much of our friendship is rooted in childhood, and when we got older, the differences in our personalities definitely stood out more, probably causing some of the friction. She's super outgoing and spontaneous and fun, and I'm introverted, quiet, and not one to like being the center of attention... and also not one to have ten best friends.

I hope that goes well. I'm meeting her for dinner after work tomorrow night. There's a Chili's near the center, and she doesn't work too far from there at her new job (which is in a doctor's office, doing medical filing or something). I am really, really hoping we can get to the bottom of this. I miss her, and frankly, I've really needed her... It sucks that I haven't had her companionship through this breakup.

Wish me luck.

XOXO,

Tessa

October

October 2nd, 1999

UGH SHE BROUGHT PETE WITH HER.

I was SO mad... but from what he said, I get the distinct feeling she didn't get a lot of say in it. He drove her to work this morning, so she didn't even have her own car. He's such a fucking controlling bastard.

When he went to the bathroom, I was like, "Van... I thought it was going to be just us!" Then she accused me of not liking him, and I can't really claim that I do, can I? So I just said, "What does that have to do with wanting to spend time ALONE with my best friend, especially when I've been through a breakup and we've barely talked?"

She didn't have an answer for that, and he came back at that moment. Then, I swear to god (which is meaningless as an atheist, but it's just a figure of speech) when SHE went to the bathroom, the fucking piece of shit came on to me... oh, it was subtle. Sort of. He put his damn hand on my thigh, and I removed it.

"What's wrong, Sexy?" he asked. "Don't like being touched?"

UGH GROSS.

"Not by you, I don't," I answered. "Do that again, and I will make sure Vanessa hears about it," I promised.

"Yeah, like she'd believe you over me," he said in response. Sadly, I know he's probably right. Even if part of her believed me, she wouldn't want to hear it or believe it, and now I am wrestling with whether or not to tell her. I mean, it's not like he made an outright proposition, but it was pretty fucking clear... and it's not the first time he's made me uncomfortable in that way.

So I don't know what to do, and now I don't want to tell her because I feel awkward. I don't want to be around HIM again, either, and apparently she's no longer allowed to have friends she spends time with alone.

Sigh. Why is life so fucking complicated?

XOXO,

Tessa

October 10th, 1999

Today is Olivia's 8th birthday, and we're celebrating by going to the Natural History Museum. She hasn't been there before, and our mom has some function to go to in the city anyway, so she's going to drop us off and pick us up later. I'm so excited. I love having time alone with my baby sister. She's such a great kid, and she always cheers me up when I'm sad.

Plus, I want to create some new memories in the city, not just ones shadowed by Mia or even Sara. Not that the memories with either are necessarily bad, but... loaded, at the least.

So I've made it a goal to get to the city on a more regular basis, even if I'm by myself. This is just the first part of that journey.

More later!

XOXO,

Tessa

October 10th, 1999 (9.10 pm)

Well, today was way more eventful than I ever could've imagined. Olivia and I had a blast at the museum. Mom called my (new) cell phone because she was running later than she expected, so I told her I'd take Olivia to dinner and through the park. It was still light out, and Livvy hadn't ever been to Central Park, so it was really fun to be the first to take her there, too.

I know a little pizza place on the Upper East Side from when I used to stay with Mia. The food is cheap and so good, so I took her there. We were sitting and eating pizza (eggplant for me, white with broccoli for her) and having a really great time together, as we always do, being goofy and silly. I wasn't obsessing over the caloric details of my pizza, which was nice since pizza is a food I often struggle with mentally (Fat Fighters "training," sadly).

We finished our pizza, and I needed to grab some lip balm, so we ducked into the Gristedes next to the pizza place. We were waiting in line to check out when I suddenly heard Olivia shout, "MIA!"

My brain just about exploded. I turned, and sure enough, in line a few customers down, holding a carton of orange juice, there stood my ex-girlfriend who, as far as I was aware, was supposed to be in Colorado.

Olivia ran from our place in line and immediately hugged Mia. This is the point at which I wanted to just vanish into thin air. To her credit, although clearly as shocked as I was, Mia bent down and gave Olivia a big hug.

I got out of the line, and so did Mia, with Olivia in tow. I had absolutely no idea what to say.

"Fancy meeting you here," is what my anxious brain eventually came up with.

"No kidding," she replied, sounding a bit breathless.

God, she looked incredible. She had on the knee-high boots I've loved since the first time I saw her wear them late last winter, with a denim skirt and a deep-red v-neck sweater, which is absolutely the most incredible color on her with her dark hair and eyes, and which naturally showed cleavage that I wish I could pretend I hadn't noticed, but of course I had.

The urge to kiss her was so strong that I'm fairly sure the only thing that kept me from doing so was Olivia's tug at my hand.

"I thought you said Mia moved away," she said, pouting.

"I did, sweetie. I was in Colorado, but I just moved back here. Your sister didn't know yet."

Moved back, as in for good? *Yet*, she'd said, and my brain noted it. As if I was going to know? Had she really just moved back? Why the fuck hadn't Ryan told me she was back? I had so many questions and not a single answer, and with Olivia there, I couldn't very well ask them.

As if on cue, my mom called right then. I told her where we were so she could pick us up, and I hung up. I put the lip balm back on a shelf and took Olivia out. Mia put her juice down and followed us.

"Tess," Mia said, hesitantly. "Is there any chance you could stay? I can get you a car home later. I'd just... I'd really like to talk to you. Please?" Her chocolate eyes were wide and imploring; how could I say no?

My mom was understandably shocked to see us with Mia, but though she looked concerned, she didn't protest when I told her that I was going to stay and "catch up" with Mia. Olivia was a little sad, but I promised her we'd go for a special birthday dessert later this week, and that appeased her.

So we walked the two blocks to Mia's apartment, she opened a bottle of wine, and we talked.

"I'm not even sure where to start," she began.

"When the hell did you get back? Last I knew, you were in Colorado for the long haul." Then I winced, because it dawned on me that her mom might have taken a turn and died suddenly. "I'm sorry. I didn't mean that to sound bitchy. It's just... is your mom..." my voice trailed off.

"She's alive. They don't think she has a lot of time left, but I'm not going back."

I was stunned.

"But what happened?"

"I told her that I wanted to try to convince you to come visit. That I missed you desperately, and that I was so very wrong to leave you in the first place. That I loved her, but I also loved you, and that you were - I hoped - my future. I asked her to please accept you, if you were even willing to speak to me, and I said that if she truly loved me, she would."

Mia stood up and began pacing. I felt my mouth hanging open but couldn't seem to close it.

"There were a lot of tears, and I thought I'd gotten through to her. She told me she loved me, and of course she accepted me. In that moment, my heart just... it's corny, but I felt like it was soaring. I mean, even if I had no hope of getting you back, even if we were truly over, just to have my mom finally, after all these years, accept that I am not straight and that I have had relationships with women, that I've loved women... it meant so much to me."

"So what happened?" I asked, when she stopped speaking and sat back down.

129

She looked anguished. Her eyes welled up with tears, and it took all of my self restraint to not take her in my arms to comfort her, but my feelings were just... well I don't even have a word for it, honestly. I was feeling so many things, so many conflicting things. Among them, perhaps strongest of all, was the absolute terror of being hurt by Mia for a third time in one year.

"When we went to sleep that night, I had planned it all out. I was going to call Ryan the next day. I knew you had been seeing each other," she added, and I felt my face get warm, but I wasn't going to defend my actions when I knew I'd done nothing wrong. Ryan helped me heal after she left me, and I don't regret it at all.

"I thought if I could get him on board, maybe he could see if you'd be willing to talk to me again. To hear me out. I was going to fly you to Colorado, if you were willing. I planned all night in my head until I fell asleep, but then everything changed when I told my mom my plans over breakfast.

"She said, 'Mia, I said I accept you, but I can't support this choice. I won't condone your lifestyle by having that woman come to my home.' I was crushed. I told her, *'Mom, that's not acceptance. That's judgment. I love her. Doesn't that mean anything to you? Don't you want me to ever have what you and Daddy had?'*"

"I take it she said no."

"Oh, it was worse than no. She told me that what you and I have, what I might have with any woman, could never be love. It's nothing but lust and depravity and sin, and she loves me, but she can't stand by and watch as I doom my soul to hell. I swear, Tessa, we've had our fights over the years about this issue, but she's never been so... well, so fucking horrible about it."

At that point, she put her head in her hands and just started to sob. I couldn't stop myself. I moved closer to her and put my arms around her.

"Oh, Mia. I'm so sorry. I can't even imagine how that

felt to hear." And I can't. My grandmother was the worst, but even she didn't say anything remotely close to that. She was just sort of vaguely snarky about it, insisting on calling Mia my "friend" instead of my "girlfriend," which is hilarious to me because my grandmother had always called all of my female friends my "girlfriends" over the years. Suddenly, that word became verboten to her.

Still, Mia gave up everything to be with her mother... her job, her life here with me, her friends. This was her mother's thanks for that? Ugh. I was so angry.

"I told her, point blank, that I couldn't believe she'd treat her only child this way. I said, 'do you even realize what I gave up to be here with you? I left behind the love of my life, and you don't even care.'"

"What did she say to that?"

Mia laughed, but it was mirthless.

"She told me she had never been so proud of me as she'd been when I told her I ended things with you to go be with her in her final days. She told me she thought that showed it wasn't really love at all, because if she'd been asked to leave my father that way, she'd never have done it. The thing is, if she HAD asked, I don't think I would've gone, but she didn't ask me to do it; I offered, and that made the hurt even worse. I walked away from you, from what we had, from our future... I did it because I thought I had to; I thought that if I didn't, I'd always feel guilty and live with regret. I guess that's true, because it's who I am, but I could've prevented all of it if only I'd laid it out for her at that time. If I had told her I'd come so she could spend her final days at home, which I knew she wanted, but that you were coming with me, or at least that you'd be visiting regularly. If only I'd had the guts to say it then, I would've known. I would've known I was risking everything for someone who truly didn't give a shit about my happiness at all."

"I don't know what to say," I said quietly, after several moments of silence.

"Oh, Tessa... there's nothing for you to say. I never should've gone. Not without you. I'm so sorry for hurting you that way. You were so supportive, and I know I broke your heart. I was scared. I was scared of confronting my mom, because on some level, I think I knew... I knew I wouldn't like what happened if I pushed, and I didn't want to lose my mom that way when I was already about to lose her to cancer. I don't know if that even makes any sense, but... yeah. Honestly, Tess, I was scared of you. I was scared of us. I worried what would happen if I didn't go, either because of you or for our relationship, and then regretted it or we broke up."

I let all of this wash over me for a few minutes and said nothing. She refilled our glasses. I sipped my wine and thought about it.

I get it now, Dear Book. When she laid it all out that way, it seemed so logical to me, so understandable. I think I'd have done some things differently, but I can't know that. No one can until they are in that situation. For all the history with my own mom, her addiction and our vastly different personalities, she accepted Mia without hesitation. My dad was just like, *oh hey, you know me and Shauna* (Wicked Stepmother #1) *did some crazy shit in our early days together*, and I was like, *ew gross, Dad, did not need that info, thanks.*

So how can I fault Mia for making the choice that felt best to her in a situation that was fairly devastating from every angle?

I told her this.

"I can't say that I don't wish you'd fought for us from the moment you got the news, because I'd be lying. I know you were agonized, though. I knew even then, even when I was most hurt and angry, that this wasn't about me, not really. It was about you and your mom, and you had to make a decision I can't even imagine given my history with my parents compared to yours with your parents.

"I would've gone with you, Mia. I think I made that as clear as I could without putting too much pressure on you at the time, but given what you've shared, I see why you didn't choose that. I was crushed. I felt like... I felt like I couldn't breathe. I was trying to hide the pain as much as I could, in part because I didn't want to feel like I was using it to manipulate your choices, but I was also afraid to let you know you had that much power over my heart."

"I know I am asking for a lot, Tess... but can you ever forgive me? Is there any chance for us? For us to start again and see what this can become?"

I hesitated, because oh god... I want that chance again. I love her. I want to be with her. But this is twice now. Twice she's run scared from me and hurt me in the process.

Can I ever trust her again?

"Mia, I'm not mad at you anymore. I don't begrudge you the choice you made. I truly don't, but..."

I paused. She leaned in, as if to kiss me. I pulled back, and honestly, Book, I have to say I am so damn proud of myself for that. I wanted to just give in to it, to let it wash over me, to feel her lips on mine again. Instead, I put my hand up.

"Don't. Please, don't. I can't. I need time, Mia. You've done this to me twice, and I know the circumstances were vastly different, and I understand fear of being hurt, but that's why I don't know. I don't know if I can ever truly trust you with my heart... with **me**... again.

"I still love you. I've never stopped, not for a second. Not when I was with Ryan, not when I was at my angriest, but I don't know if it's enough right now. I just don't."

Silent tears ran down her beautiful face, and it just killed me to be the source of them, even though I knew my feelings were entirely justified. I picked up my purse.

"I think I should go," I told her quietly. She nodded.

"Okay. I get it. I do. I don't know if I could give me another chance, either, but I promise you, Tessa... I won't do this to you again. I will never run away from what we can become again. If you can't give me the chance to prove that, I'll respect it. I'll leave you alone, but please know that I will forever regret that I cost myself the most incredible thing that has ever happened to me. I'll never stop loving you," she said, with a small hiccup of a sob.

I walked out her door, and I didn't look back.

Because if I had... I'd have melted into her arms without thinking twice.

I really, really need to think right now. I want desperately to just act. I want to get on a train back to the city right now.

I want Mia. I've wanted Mia my entire life, but I don't know if I can take this risk. In a year that's been all about me being brave, can I do this? The most daring, bravest thing I'll have ever had to do?

XOXO,

Tessa

October 12th, 1999

I went out with Ryan tonight, but only for dinner. With Mia back, I've put the brakes on our sexual relationship. I didn't even need to tell him that; he knew it was a game-changer.

He's known Mia a lot longer than I have, and I really wanted his insight, but even more than that, he's my friend. I know that despite his friendship with Mia, he isn't going to sugarcoat things for me.

It turns out Mia hadn't told him she was coming back. She'd been back only a few days when I ran into her, and she hadn't yet called him. I guess she was still processing what her mother had said and done, along with whether or not she should try to reach out to me.

"Tess, do you want to be with her? I mean really with her. Not like before, where it was first about intellectual chemistry and lust, or the early stages of your romantic relationship when everything was shiny and new. You've seen the ugly now. You know Mia can run scared from things sometimes. I've seen her do it, but I also can tell you that in all the years I've known her, she's never broken a promise to me - and she makes them rarely. That matters, in my opinion."

"It matters to me, too. I never really understood the value of keeping a promise before I met the two of you, but neither of you has ever misled me or given me false hope. You've both been honest, even when it was hard, and even when it hurt. That's been something I keep coming back to... I've been abandoned all of my life. I've been let down by literally everyone who ever should've been there for me, often when I needed them most. That's family and friends. I called Vanessa the other day and left her a message about Mia, and she hasn't called me back yet. That hurts, too."

We sat in silence for a bit and ate our dinners. I kept feeling like he was on the verge of talking, but then he'd stop, so I finally pressed him.

"What is it, Ry? You want to say something, and you're not."

"Look, Tessa, I know you're still in love with her. I know she's still in love with you. She put her relationship with her mom - who is dying - on the line for another chance with you. She knew she might not get it. She even told me she figured it was incredibly unlikely, but she did it, and for me that says a lot. She also needed to know for herself how her mom was going to react to her ultimatum, but I honestly think it was more about wanting you back than anything else. I feel like that has to count for something. It just speaks volumes to me."

"How had I not thought of it that way?" I murmured. "You're totally fucking right, and I somehow missed that completely."

"I thought you might have, which is why I decided I needed to point it out. Tess, she means it. I really believe her. I've never seen her this way about anyone else. Even Taylor, and they were together a long time."

"Ryan, were you... did you ever love her? I mean, I know you love her, but did you *love her* love her?" I asked awkwardly. I'm not sure why I'd never thought to ask it before, but something about the way he was telling me all of this made me wonder.

"Yeah. I did. When we were first together, it was casual, but I fell for her pretty hard. She wasn't in love with me, though. It was tough at first, to just be friends. We still hooked up now and then, as you well know, but by then, I was no longer in love with her, and it was easier. Besides, I was enamored with you at that point."

"Me? Wait, what?"

"Really, Tess? You had no idea I had started to fall for you?" he asked. "You really don't have any idea the effect you can have on people, do you?" he added, with a hint of sorrow in his voice.

"No. I had no idea. I'm sorry."

"There's nothing to be sorry about, Tessa. You never made me any proclamations or promises, either. I never felt misled by you, and besides that, you met Mia right around the time I was falling for you. I could see immediately that there was something there, that it was more than sex. I knew that night we were all together that she was going to fall for you in a way she hadn't for me, and you had a crush on her before you even met her, although I do admit that it initially had made me wonder if it was just lust on your end. By the end of that weekend in Vermont, I was pretty damn sure you two were going to be together, and if I couldn't have either of you in that way,

I wished for you two to have each other. I was your silent cheerleader all along," he said with a smile.

I was dumbstruck. While he hadn't come out and said he'd fallen in love with me completely, this made three people over the past year who had loved me - that way - or at least in Ryan's case, come close to loving me. Was he right? Am I special in some way I've never realized?

I thought about the poem I'd read the day I met Sara. Some part of me knew this about myself all along. Not in an "oh, I'm so amazing," toss my hair, full-of-myself kind of way, but in a quiet, surprisingly self-assured, *I am worthy* way.

We finished dinner, and he brought me home. I've been sitting here staring at the phone ever since. I can't decide if I should call Mia or not.

Since it's been an hour, I'm going to wait. I see Claire tomorrow night, and I have to share all of this with her before I act. I just need to get the perspective of someone clinical and detached.

XOXO,
Tessa

October 13th, 1999

I just got back from seeing Claire, and I caught her up on all of it. Perhaps the most surprising thing she had to say was when she smiled and told me, "Tessa, even I strongly suspected Ryan was half in love with you, just based on what you shared about your relationship with him."

I hadn't expected that, but when I think about the way he touched me, the way he held me, the way he made love to me (and yeah, fucked me), I've only had anything even remotely like that with two other people... Sara and Mia, both of whom told me they were in love with me.

I'm glad that I reconnected with Sara because I'd felt really guilty about hurting her and breaking her heart. I know I didn't lead her on, but I still feel like I should've been more careful with her. She seems happy now, and I think she's over me, which is reassuring. She deserves it because she truly is an incredible human being. I want her to be happy. I wanted her to be happy with me, frankly, but I just couldn't be that person for her. It wouldn't have been fair to either of us to pretend that I could.

Ryan's given me his support and encouragement, and he wants me to be happy, too. He thinks that could happen with Mia.

So I told Claire that I want to be happy with Mia. I want to believe her. I want to dive in and never look back.

"Then what's stopping you?" she asked. "Only you can make you happy. You have to decide what you want and then decide if it's worth fighting for it."

"I'm scared," I finally said, tears burning my eyes. "I'm afraid of losing her, again."

"But right now you don't have her at all, Tessa. Is that really better?"

No, it's not.

So... it's time to pick up the phone and take the next step in my journey with Mia.

It's time to find that same courage that led me to her in the first damn place.

XOXO,
Tessa

November

November 2nd, 1999

Dear Book,

I know it's been a while, but I've been... preoccupied. Yes, with Mia. I took the chance and laid it all out on the line.

"I can't ever do this again," I told her. "So it has to be all or nothing this time, Mia. I mean it. I love you. I love you so goddamn much that it hurts to think of losing you a third time, but you promised me you would not run scared, and I am going to take the chance and trust you. If I don't, I'll hate myself for it forever."

She promised again and told me she loved me. We were together the very next night. She surprised me at work, arriving with peach roses, my favorite flowers. I was in my "uniform" with spit-up on my shirt from one of the babies who has reflux, and my hair was a freakin' nightmare. She just walked up to me and kissed me in the parking lot and told me I was beautiful and that she was so happy I'd agreed to give us another chance.

We've been virtually inseparable since that night. I've slept home maybe four nights that entire time. I've been reverse commuting to Clark for work every day, stopping briefly at home after to see Olivia (who has been a bit emotional about my absence) and then heading back to New York.

Tonight, I'm sleeping at home so my mom can work the night shift at the diner. I miss Mia so much already that it aches.

Is it completely crazy to consider moving in with her already? The reverse commute is brutal, and I've been exhausted, though also exhilarated.

It's too soon, a voice in my head keeps whispering.

Says who, answers another.

In other news, I finally talked to Vanessa. We HAD mostly patched things up, but then I was on AIM talking to her the other night from Mia's, trying to set up plans for all of us to get together... and the fucking rat bastard messaged me on the side.

BigPete69 *(yes, that's his username)*: Hey, Sexy.

Tessca22 *(Tessca is a name one of my students used to call me)*: You have to stop calling me that.

BigPete69: Why? You ARE sexy, Sexy *("Oh, how original, Pete. Seriously, I'm creaming in my pants right now," I thought)*.

Tessca22: Because you're with my best friend, and I'm not going to hurt her, and I'd like you to stop hurting her.

BigPete69: How am I hurting her? It's just a joke.

Tessca22: Fuck you, Pete. Yeah, sure it's just a "joke" to you. Everything is a joke to you, but

Vanessa's not a goddamn joke to me.
I love her, and I'm not going to
just sit around and let you treat
her this way without standing up for
both myself and her. So, seriously,
just fuck you. Vanessa deserves more
than this. Someday, she'll figure
that out, and I'll be so fucking
glad when she does and you're
history.

Then Mia caught wind of what was going on, and she was fucking LIVID. I've seriously never seen her so angry. She took over the keyboard to talk to him herself.

Tessca22: Pete, this is Mia… Tessa's
girlfriend. You need to fuck off.
She's made it crystal fucking clear
she's NOT interested, and you've
put your fucking hands on her when
you're with another woman, who, OH
YEAH, IS HER BEST FUCKING FRIEND.
Leave Tessa alone… I'm fucking
serious. I have no qualms about
outing you, unlike my girlfriend,
who's too nice for her own good in
this case.

BigPete69: Oooh, a girlfriend getting
feisty. HOT SHIT. What are you
wearing?

At that point, Mia logged off my account. She printed the conversation.

"Tess, I know you don't want to be the bad guy, but you HAVE to tell her. Vanessa has a right to know." She handed me the printout.

"Ugh, I know. I'm just afraid she won't believe it, even with this."

So now I have plans to see Vanessa on Saturday, and Mia's coming. We're both hoping Pete won't show his face, but I suspect he will.

I just hope Van believes me and not him... for her sake, as well as for the sake of our friendship.

XOXO,
Tessa

Novewber 6th, 1999

Dinner with Van last night was quite the affair. As I expected, Pete did show up. Mia said, "that piece of shit has quite the pair, doesn't he?" to which I replied, "yeah and I'd like to take care of that for him, and not in a way he'd enjoy." Which made her laugh.

That's more or less where the laughter ended.

Much to my incredulity, when Vanessa got to our table, she immediately hugged me, told Mia how glad she was to finally meet her, and then thrust out her hand. Yeah. Her left hand.

Which had a fucking engagement ring on it.

Ughhhh.

Mia and I looked at each other, and I just sat there, speechless. Van misinterpreted that and said, "I know! I was completely surprised by it, too!"

I took a sip of water.

"Wh- when did you propose?" I asked Pete.

"Oh, the other night," he said... with a motherfucking wink.

In other words, the night Mia and I called him out on his shit.

"It was so romantic," Vanessa gushed. "I'd gone to bed, as you know, and he came in and he just knelt by the side of the bed, took my hand, and said, 'Vanessa Banfield, I love you. Will you be my forever?'"

At this point, Pete took her hand. I wanted to vomit. "And she said yes, of course," he added. "I went out and bought her the ring the next day."

Then he kissed her, but although her eyes closed, his did not, and he made a point of looking over at me. And I swear to god, Book... I saw that bastard smirk.

The dinner was awkward and 10,000 kinds of uncomfortable. I had the printout in my purse. Mia and I kept looking at each other, but we were both so stunned that I don't think either of us was sure of what to do.

So I excused myself and said I needed to use the restroom, kind of nodding for Mia to come with me. Unfortunately, Van also came with us.

"Oh my god," she said in a rush, once we were out of earshot. "I can't believe I'm getting married."

Oh my god, I thought. *Neither can I.*

"How long have you two been together?" Mia asked.

"Since I was 19, so five years almost," she answered.

She was so goddamn jubilant. How on earth could I burst her bubble?

I have rarely felt so fucking trapped. I know he's a bastard. I feel it in my gut. I know he's going to cheat on her (if he hasn't already), and I know he's going to hurt her (which he definitely has already).

But how do you crush your best friend's dream that way?

In the end, I just couldn't do it. Mia completely understood my paralysis on the matter.

"I don't think I could've done it, either, baby," she told me on the way back to her apartment.

I can't just let her marry him... right? I mean, what kind of friend am I if I do?

UGH

FUCKING UGH.

XOXO,

Last night, I went out with Vanessa and Pete, this time without Mia as a buffer. As a test, when Van went to use the ladies' room, I stayed at the table.

And oh boy, did he fucking fail.

"You thought you had me, huh?" he asked, almost immediately.

"What are you talking about?"

"I know you and Mia were planning to try to break us up. You can't. She'll choose me over you. I know it, and you know it. Besides, we both know you secretly want me. Otherwise, you'd have already told her about me."

"Uhm, what are you fucking smoking, Pete? Because I so DO NOT want you," I replied furiously. "All I want from you is to fucking not break my best friend's heart, but it's too late for that."

"So then why not just give into it?" he said, and he took my hand. The motherfucking piece of shit dared to touch me.

I snatched my hand away. "Do not ever fucking touch me again, and let me make this crystal fucking clear... you and I are NEVER happening, Pete. NEVER."

He put his foot on my leg under the table, at which point I lost my fucking shit completely, and I took MY foot and dug my wedge heel into his groin.

He cried out in pain and swore.

"What the fuck is wrong with you?" he yelled. Several people turned to look at us, and unfortunately for me, Vanessa chose that moment to come back.

"What's going on?" she asked, looking alarmed.

"Your friend just assaulted me," Pete said, his face bright red. "She put her foot in my crotch, and when I told her to get it the fuck off me, she dug her damn heel into my balls."

"Oh my god! That is not what happened, you lying

144

piece of shit."

"What?! Tess, what the fuck?"

"Vanessa, listen... you need to understand. It's not what it sounds like."

"It sounds like you were coming on to my fiance," she said, and I knew this was not going to end well at that moment.

"Van, I'm with Mia. You know I'm with Mia, that I love her completely."

Pete snorted. "Yeah, right."

"Fuck you," I said. "Vanessa, he's been making subtle come-ons for months. I ignored it because I didn't want it to be true. I told myself I was imagining it, but I knew I wasn't. When you went to bed the night he proposed to you, he started up on AIM, and Mia told him off. We were going to tell you at dinner, but then he came with you, and you had your big announcement, and well... I chickened out," I admitted.

"What is she talking about, Pete? What did you do?"

"All I did was teasingly call her sexy, babe. I was just being NICE because, let's face it, she's really so not sexy. I just wanted to give her an ego-boost so maybe she wouldn't be so goddamn jealous of your happiness."

"Oh. My. God. He's a fucking pathological liar, Vanessa. I have proof."

I dug out the printed conversation and passed it to her. She read it and started to cry.

Pete snatched it from her and told her flat out that it was faked.

"Clearly, she and that girlfriend of hers are trying to end us. Look, Tessa, I'm sorry I rejected your overtures, but I am in love with Vanessa, and you can't come between us."

At that point, I started to cry.

"Van, c'mon... we've been friends for so long. Would I ever do anything even remotely like this? You know me, Vanessa. You know I love you and would never hurt you this way." *Please, please believe me*, I pleaded silently.

"Honestly, Tessa I don't know anything right now. I can't believe you kept this from me, if it's all true. So why should I believe you now? Pete's never lied to me before," she said, and god, I had to bite my tongue to keep from saying, *except for all the times you've told me he has...* but I knew that wouldn't help, so I held back.

"C'mon babe, let's get out of here. You don't deserve a friend like this bitch," Pete said, standing up. He grabbed her hand and kissed it. "You know I love you. You know I'd never hurt you."

He pulled her to his chest, and goddamn it if she didn't embrace him back. I couldn't believe what was happening, except he'd set me up so perfectly. I knew he was scum, but I didn't realize he was so devious, too. To be honest, I didn't think he had two brain cells to rub together.

"Vanessa, please... don't go," I pleaded. "Let's talk about this. Please."

"I can't. I just can't." She threw the printed conversation back at me. It landed on the remnants of my dinner, and she walked out.

The bastard fucking left me with the entire bill, just to add salt to the wound. I didn't have enough cash to cover it, and I don't have any credit cards. And they were supposed to be my ride home. It's freezing out there tonight.

I sat there and sobbed, trying not to make more of a spectacle of myself.

Then, I called Mia, who came to my rescue. She called me a cab and gave the manager her credit card info after telling her my sad story.

The manager, who had overheard some of what happened when a couple of other diners complained, apparently believed my side of it because she actually came over and told me she wasn't going to charge me (or rather Mia) for their food. So I just paid my own part, and I went outside to wait for my cab.

When I got home, I foolishly tried to call Vanessa. Pete answered, told me to fuck off, said never to call there again, and then hung up on me.

Now I'm home, in bed, feeling fucking destroyed.

XOXO,

Tessa

November 15th, 1999

I couldn't go to work today. I know I should've, but I barely slept, and I am utterly exhausted. I just couldn't face it.

I keep waiting for the phone to ring or for an alarm to go off to wake me from this nightmare. We've had fights over the years, like all friends, but never anything like this. Never over a guy. Even when I got mad at her ex-boyfriends who treated her like dirt, she didn't get mad at ME. She was always grateful I had her back, even if she didn't listen to me and had to learn the hard way.

I don't know, Book. I think I may have lost her this time.

Mia's called me twice today, just to check on me. She wanted me to come to the city tonight, but I can't; I promised my mom I'd babysit. So she insisted she was coming here, and I couldn't talk her out of it, even when I told her Nate was home and would probably live up to his reputation of being a fucking brat (to say the least).

"I can handle it," she assured me. "Teenage boys have never scared me."

I don't doubt her for a minute, but I still feel guilty subjecting her to his assholery, especially after the fiasco with Pete.

"Tessa, just let me love you, won't you?" she finally

said.

"How can I say no to that?" I replied, smiling for the first time in a day.

She's on her way here now. Olivia's doing her homework, and Nate's being a douche about it, saying he's going to "tell on me," like I'm 13 or something.

"I already told Mommy she's coming, so feel free to try," I said. He hadn't expected that and went down to his room in the basement to sulk.

I'm sure he'll be back to cause trouble, but I don't give a shit. I need Mia tonight, and Olivia's really excited to see her. She already asked if Mia can read to her before she goes to bed. So Nate can get stuffed.

I'm not letting another asshole boy fuck my mood up tonight.

XOXO,

Tessa

November 22nd, 1999

I can't believe it's already almost Thanksgiving. I've been writing in you for nearly a year, and you're almost out of pages, which makes me sad. You're like a friend at this point, which I rationally know is stupid, but the truth is, I've never journaled consistently for this long in my life.

Even though I still haven't heard from Vanessa, I am grateful and thankful for a lot this year. It's been brutal in some ways, but I feel like I've grown so much (and ugh, I hate how cheesy that sounds). Mia and I have been going strong without even a blip since we got back together, and I'm just so happy in that respect.

We haven't talked about moving in together, but I am

ready if she asks. When she asks. Hell, at this point, I am so far gone that if she proposed, I'd say yes in a heartbeat. Even though I know it wouldn't be "legal," I don't care. I want to spend the rest of my life with Mia Alice Forrester, and I am going to change my name to Tessa Forrester even if I have to go to court and pay legal fees to do it.

Once she did tell me she really liked the idea of being Mia Alexander, so maybe she'd change her name. Or we could be modern and hyphenate, although Forrester-Alexander is a bit of a mouthful, haha.

Regardless, the bottom line is that I am completely, totally in this relationship. I believe in it. I believe in us. We've been through so much, and we keep coming out stronger.

As for Van, I hope she'll come around. I plan to call her (because fuck Pete's wishes) on Thanksgiving. Even if she won't speak to me, I have to try.

We're going to my grandparents' house, as usual, and I already told my grandmother I am bringing Mia. I expected her to say no, but to my shock, she just kind of huffed. I'm not spending our first Thanksgiving apart, so it was either I bring Mia or I go to New York to be with her.

In some ways, I'm sorry to subject Mia to my family that way, but then again, it might be better that she knows what she's signing up for...

XOXO,
Tessa

Thanksgiving Day, 1999

Well, it's a fucking Thanksgiving miracle. First off, we got through dinner without anyone being obnox-

149

ious, which given my family's general dynamic, is a bit of a miracle. My grandmother only said about five passive-aggressive things to Mia, and my grandfather, mercifully, was - or pretended to be - oblivious even though Mia and I held hands multiple times during the day.

Even Nate behaved himself for once.

And then, the whipped cream on my pumpkin pie? Vanessa showed up. She was at her parents' house, across the street, and she came over and rang the bell. Of course, she was invited in and had pie with us. I noticed immediately that she wasn't wearing the ring, and I got really hopeful. When she finished her pie, she thanked my grandparents, then asked me if we could talk.

We went out back and stood by the pool (about as far from prying ears as you can get around there). The cover is frozen over and the float thing is (as always) already deflating, but being near the source of so many happy childhood memories with Van gave me hope.

"Tess, I'm so sorry. I never should've doubted you," she said. I started to cry... I was just so relieved.

"I should've tried to tell you sooner what had happened with Pete. It was just so nebulous at first, and part of me thought I was overreacting or even imagining it. I didn't really have any proof, and at that point, I really only even had a gut feeling to go on. You guys have been together a long time, and I was scared. I didn't want to hurt you, either."

"You didn't, but he did. I caught him last night. It turns out it wasn't just you he was flirting with. Remember my friend Samantha?"

I groaned. I never liked Samantha. She was possessive and petty.

"Oh yeah, I remember her."

"Well, as it turns out, they've apparently been fucking each other for most of the past year."

"Holy shit... Oh, my god. I'm sorry, Vanessa. I really am. I didn't want to be right, I swear."

150

"I know. None of it is your fault. He put you in an awkward position, and he played me. Big time."

"So how did you catch him?"

"He thought I was sleeping here last night, and I was going to because my mom wanted help with dinner, but... I don't know, I just felt like something was off with him, and I kept thinking of what you said. He was really kind of like feeling me out to be sure of my plans, and he claimed it was because he had a surprise for me. At first, I thought he was going to go get us a Christmas tree or something, but I just felt weird, so I went home after my mom went to bed."

"And?" I asked.

"And I saw Samantha's car in the driveway, which I found really weird at first, but then I just had a feeling... so I went in as quietly as I could, and sure enough, there they were in OUR bed. She was naked, on her knees, with his dick in her mouth."

"Fuck..."

"Yeah. So... I took off the ring, stormed over to the window, opened it, and threw the fucking thing out."

"Whoa, seriously?"

"Yep. I told him he could get his bitch to go hunt it down since she clearly likes being on her knees so much."

I couldn't help but laugh a bit at that, because it was **such** a Vanessa move.

"Oh my god. I'm sorry... and sorry for laughing, but I wish I could've seen their faces."

"Yeah, well... if you hadn't told me, I probably wouldn't have gone back there last night, so don't be sorry, okay? I'm the asshole. I never should've doubted you, even for a second. I know you never liked Pete, and I let that fuck with my judgment. That, and I just didn't want to be wrong, not after so many years together."

"I'm just glad you know now and that you found out before the wedding."

"Oh, you and me both. Anyway, I am moving out. It

means moving back to my parents' temporarily, but oh well. My mom's less than thrilled, which pisses me off because what the fuck? Am I supposed to stay with a cheating, lying piece of shit?"

"Yeah, but sadly that's your mom for you," I said.

"I know. I never understand why I expect more from her."

"You know, you and Mia have more in common than you even realize. When Mia told her mother about me, she was awful about it. Plus, her ex-fiance cheated on her.

"I'm so sorry. I haven't been there for you, Tessa. You've always, always had my back, and I should've had yours. I got so caught up in Pete's bullshit, and I let him manipulate me into thinking things I really should've known better than to believe. Not just about you, either," she added.

"I know, but Van, you were young when you met him, and you'd been through so much already. I am not angry. I mean, I was. I was really hurt, but I know he was playing you. I'm just so fucking relieved you caught him and it's over now, before he could hurt you any more."

"Me, too. It hurts, and I know when the pissed-off goes away, I'm going to be fucking devastated, but right now, I'm basically just furious. But, I really want to get to know Mia better, and I hope you'll both give me that chance."

I told her that we'd like nothing more, and then we hugged. I walked her back to her parents' house, and we said goodnight. I came back, and Mia was eagerly waiting for the details.

XOXO,
Tessa

November 30th, 1999

I saw Claire tonight, and we caught up on everything that's been going on in the past week. I told her
how relieved I was about Vanessa. Not just because I
have my friend back, but I also didn't want her to marry that douchebag and get even more hurt. Now she has
a chance to find something real with someone who will
cherish her.

"Do you feel like you've found that?" Claire asked me.

"Without a doubt," I answered without hesitation. "I
feel like I've come so goddamn far this past year, and I
think back to almost a year ago when I was feeling lost
and empty and desperate... when I was obsessing about
calories and food constantly instead of being out there
in the world, living my life. All I ever felt were cravings,
a constant need that was never satisfied, and all because
I couldn't let myself believe I deserved to feel, well... I
guess *full*, literally or metaphorically speaking."

"And now?"

"I've never felt so satiated. In every possible respect.
Sexually, emotionally, physically... I am still dealing with
some of the fallout of all of this. It's not easy to just look
in the mirror and say, *okay this is my body. It's fat, but
who cares,* but I'm doing it. It's also not easy to come to
terms with all the ways people who should've been there
for me have let me down, and often still do."

"What do you mean by that?"

"Well," I said, biting my lip. "Like my relationship
with my mom is a good example. I've always longed for
a mom who was... more demonstrative, more affection-
ate, and I always felt like my mom is kind of emotionally
distant. When she was still using, I blamed that. When
she got sober, I thought it would change. That suddenly
she'd be more open with her feelings, but that's just not
who she is. She can't help who she is any more than I can

change wanting that type of relationship with my mom, but it's not fair of me to expect her to be something she just... isn't."

"That's an interesting perspective on it," Claire said. "I think it's very astute of you to realize that."

"I mean, I can't say it isn't still hard sometimes, but I love my mom. I wanted her to accept me for who I am, so don't I kind of owe her the same in return?"

"I suppose that's fair," she replied, "as long as you remember that you have a right to get your emotional needs met from that relationship, even if that doesn't look how you wish it did." Then she asked how things were going with Mia.

"Things are amazing. I'm ready to take it to the next step. I'm ready to move in with her, to be with her fully in every respect."

At that point, our time was up, but I left feeling a sense of lightness I haven't felt in a very, very long time. If ever.

XOXO,

Tessa

December

December 1st, 1999

We've come full circle, back to December, my dearest Book. Last year at this time, before I'd gotten you, obviously, I was deeply unsettled, unsatisfied with every aspect of my life.

This year, I am so happy. Life is going amazingly well. I'm happy with myself, with my relationship. I'm... at peace, if not entirely happy with my family. I've been buying gifts for Olivia, and I plan to spoil her rotten, because I know it's going to be very hard on her when I leave, and I know I'll be moving out soon. No, Mia hasn't asked yet, but I just know it's coming.

I filled out an application to start college next fall. Mia is 100% supportive. In fact, her (early) Christmas gift to me was a check to pay off the loan I'd defaulted on after I flunked out of Trenton State all those years ago. I burst into tears when she gave it to me. I'm thinking of studying psychology. For a long time, I wanted to be a teacher, but now I'm thinking maybe a school psychologist instead. We'll see. I'm just excited by the prospect of being in school again.

As much as I love the babies I take care of every day, and as fond as I am of (most of) their parents, I am also exhausted by it all at this point. I'm ready for the next chapter in my life, in basically every respect.

I'm thinking I may give my notice that I'm leaving after December 31st. I don't have another job lined up yet, not officially, but there's an adorable baby girl in Mia's building, and I've struck up a friendship with her mom, Cassidy, who is going back to work after the New Year. She had mentioned in passing that she was looking for a nanny, and wouldn't that be convenient when I move in with Mia? I told her I was potentially interested and gave her some of my references, and we'll see. I have a good feeling about it.

I am full of good feelings right now, and it's just so fucking nice to feel this way.

XOXO,

Tessa

December 5th, 1999

Today is a sad day for my poor Mia. Her mom died last night. The hospice called her this morning, and I held her while she cried. It broke my heart because at one point, she sobbed, "why couldn't she just love me for me?"

I had no answer for her.

We knew this was coming. She's been in hospice since before Thanksgiving. I asked Mia if she wanted to go see her to say goodbye, but when Mia called her and told her she wanted to come say goodbye but wouldn't come without me, her mother told her she didn't want her dying memory of her daughter to be with the "harlot" who was condemning her to hell. While it made me sad, it also made me happy to hear Mia laugh and say, "Mom... who the fuck uses the word harlot anymore?" before she said, "Goodbye then, Mother. I'm sorry you can't see past your hatred, because Tessa is amazing. I love you, despite everything."

And she hung up. That was the last time they spoke, and Mia seems at peace with it for the most part, even if she's also still deeply hurt. I asked her if she's considered therapy, because to be honest, I feel like it would help her process all of this, and she said she has and might go, especially after seeing how much it's helped me this year.

Speaking of which, I have my last session with Claire tomorrow. I don't expect to be in Cranford a lot longer, and frankly, I'm barely here now. I've spent most nights with Mia, and it's just time for me to move on. I can't imagine it's my last dance with a therapist, but I feel like Claire's taken me as far as she can. I have all the tools I need, at least for now, and I know how to use them to make my life better, to keep... well *living*. Finally. It took me long enough, but Claire pointed out that some people sadly never get there at all. I know that firsthand. I've seen it in most of my family members.

That's why I was so damn determined to break the chains, to break the damn cycle.

And fuck if I haven't managed to do just that.

XOXO,

Tessa

December 12th, 1999

Well, it's official! Tonight, Mia asked me to move in with her. Actually, she didn't ask, exactly. We'd just finished having some especially phenomenal sex (even by

157

our standards), and we were naked and snuggled up on her bed when she handed me a wrapped box.

"Mia! You've already given me my gift!" I protested.

"Just open it," she said, breathlessly.

It was my key on the Tiffany keychain she gave me before her mom got sick. Or at least I thought it was, but then she told me to turn it over.

When I did, my eyes teared up. *I promise to love you forever. Move in with me?*

I kissed her in response, and the key was quickly put aside.

So on January 2nd, I am moving in with Mia. I told her I need to spend one last New Year's Eve with Olivia, and she totally understood. She's going to join me in New Jersey for this one. Everyone's all abuzz about Y2K (which has me rolling my eyes) so she figured it might not be a terrible idea to leave the city. "Just in case," she said.

"Besides, there's no way in hell I am not kissing you at midnight," she added, at which point I confessed that I'd never been kissed at midnight on New Year's Eve.

She kissed me and said, "consider that a downpayment."

XOXO,

Tessa

December 14th, 1999

Today started off great. Last night, Cassidy called to ask me if I'd be Hannah's nanny, and I said yes without hesitation. I told her I was moving in with Mia on January 2nd, but that for all intents and purposes, the date was a formality, and I'll be mostly moved in before New

Year's.

I gave notice at work today. Michelle, the current director, actually teared up a little. That got me all teary, and I already know it's going to be so hard to leave these babies I love so much. I asked her to let me write a goodbye letter to the parents, and she agreed, so I'll do that this weekend, and she'll give it to them next week.

I came home and told my mom. I haven't really had the chance because she worked last night, and I had gotten home right before she'd left. She surprised me by crying, but she also kind of rained on my parade a little by saying that she was "worried" because Mia and I have had so many ups and downs. I told her I was sure; I knew this was the right move for me and for our relationship.

Then I had to tell Olivia, and oh, god... that was gut-wrenching. She clung to me, and she cried, and she begged me not to go. Leaving her is so goddamn hard for me. I wish I could take her with me. I always say that she's the child of my heart, my "sisterchild," and I mean it, but I also know she's NOT actually mine and that I can't take her with me no matter how desperately I wish I could.

I told her that she can come and visit me and Mia all the time and spend long weekends there and some time in the summer. I promised her we'd do things together and that I would come back to visit regularly.

"Every day?" she asked, through her tears.

"No, sweetheart, not every day, but I haven't been here every day for a while now, either."

"I know," she said, sadly, "and I miss you."

I hugged her. "I miss you, too, Olivia, but I will always be here for you," I said. "Me leaving to be with Mia won't change how much I love you, and Mia loves you, too, so it's almost like you're getting another sister."

She sniffled and just clung to me. After that, I tucked her in, came into my room, and cried for an hour on the phone with Mia. I begged her to understand that it isn't that I don't want to live with her. I'm just brokenhearted that it means leaving my little Olivia behind.

"Oh, Tess... I'm sorry, love. I know what she means to you. I wish she could come with you."

"Somehow, I don't think our mom would approve of that," I said with a half laugh, "and as much as part of me wants to bring her with me, I also know that I have the right to my own life and that I have to live it freely because no matter how my heart feels, at the end of the day, she isn't my daughter. Frankly, it will probably be good for her and my mom... they'll get a chance to bond more without me here."

That's what I hope for them, anyway. I want them to have that closeness. For both of their sakes.

XOXO,
Tessa

December 17th, 1999

Mia never ceases to surprise me. Tonight, she took me out to get a tree. A live one, from a corner deli (of all places, but that's NYC for you). We stopped at CVS first to buy lights and some ornaments. She has some from her childhood, but she said she wanted to make new memories with me. I even found one of the Hallmark "Our First Christmas Together" ornaments. It's silver with a red ribbon, and I love it, even if we're not "officially" living together yet. We'll be spending Christmas Eve together, and I think that counts. Mia just laughed and told me I was adorable before kissing me.

It turns out she did all of this for one very sneaky reason. See, I'd told her in Vermont when we were making out by the fireplace that I've always wanted to have sex on the floor, beneath the lights of a Christmas tree... and she wanted to give me that dream tonight.

So we decorated while listening to Christmas music and drinking cocoa spiked with peppermint Schnapps. When we were done, while the tree was, uhm, admittedly a tad sparsely decorated, it still looked beautiful to me.

Mia grabbed her down comforter and told me to get pillows off the bed and couch. We made a little nest beside the tree, and she told me that she wanted to unwrap me, that I was the best present she could ever find under her tree.

Then we both giggled at how corny that sounded, but through her laughter, she insisted it was still true.

She proceeded to very, very slowly undress me, kissing every inch of skin as she exposed it. I was writhing in anticipation by the time she got my pants off, desperate to feel her fingers moving inside of me. I arched against her palm as she cupped my breast.

"Oh, Mia," I whispered. "I love you so much."

She leaned over me, her sleek hair tickling my bare breasts as she did.

"I love you, Tessa," she whispered back.

I flipped her over and straddled her, and I began to caress her through her clothes. She moaned as I unzipped her jeans and slipped them off her hips, my fingers dipping into her thong as I did. I kissed her neck and slowly unbuttoned her top. Her full breasts were covered by her lacy bra, but her nipples were hard and visible through the sheer red fabric. I leaned forward and gently bit one, my mouth closing over it, without having removed her bra. I slipped a finger into her warmth and felt her muscles clamp down around it. I kissed her as she came, her beautiful face aglow in the lights of the tree while Karen Carpenter sang *Merry Christmas, Darling* on the CD player.

"You've never been more beautiful," I whispered against her lips.

"Neither have you," she replied. "Now... your turn."

She kissed her way down my belly, and it vaguely occurred to me that once I'd have recoiled at that. My anxieties and insecurities would've interfered with my pleasure in this moment, a moment I'd wanted for so many years, but it was fleeting, and all I felt was... glorious.

Mia's tongue flicked across my clit, and I cried out as she sucked it into her mouth, coming almost instantly, even before she slid her fingers inside me. She moved them quickly, and before I knew it, I had come again... and again.

Finally, she came back up and kissed me, and I wrapped her in my arms. We fell asleep under a fuzzy blanket in the afterglow of our lovemaking, beneath the glimmer of the Christmas tree's lights.

It was the perfect fantasy come true.

XOXO,

Tessa

December 19th, 1999

Tonight, Mia threw an impromptu Christmas party, inviting Ryan and a few other friends, most of whom I hadn't met before. We spend most of our time alone. We're both introverts, and anyway, we really don't like sharing each other (which is sort of amusing, considering we shared each other with Ryan that first weekend, but I digress). After some internal debate, I asked her if she'd mind if I invited Sara and Sasha, and she told me it was completely fine with her.

Honestly, I wasn't totally sure if Sara would come, but she did, and I'm happy to say it wasn't at all awkward. She and Mia got on really well together, which was nice.

Sara seems really happy with Sasha, and she confessed to me privately that she's in love with her and that they're talking about going to Ukraine, although Sasha's parents are pretty conservative. I told her she should have Sasha talk to Mia about that, since Mia certainly understands that experience, and in ways neither Sara nor I can, having been fortunate enough to have accepting parents (at least in this regard).

It was a fabulous night. We had great takeout from Lili's, (which has the most amazing noodles ever), we baked cookies (okay, so maybe they were premade dough, but we did add sprinkles and icing!), and we had eggnog and talked about how we both really don't love eggnog and yet can't seem to help but have one glass every year.

We hadn't seen Ryan together since, well... before the breakup. I was afraid that would be awkward, too, but he was genuinely warm and gave us a "moving in together/Christmas" gift. It turned out to be an engraved plaque that said "Alexander/Forrester Home, 2000." I protested that her name should've gone first, since it's her place, but he said I was first alphabetically, and we both laughed at him. It was sweet, though, and we both love it.

After talking and playing a game of Scrabble (which Ryan won), we decided to watch *It's A Wonderful Life*, and at one point during the movie, I cheesily whispered to Mia, *thanks to your love, it IS a wonderful life.*

She leaned into me, and we snuggled together for the rest of the movie. After the movie ended, people slowly began to say goodnight and left. By 10pm, it was just us, and we finally fell asleep in each other's arms around midnight.

It was the most amazing weekend... one of the very best of my entire life.

XOXO,

Tessa

Christmas Eve, 1999

I took off yesterday and today so I could have a four-day weekend to enjoy Christmas with Mia, Olivia, and the rest of my family. I slept at Mia's last night, and she came with me to my mom's for Christmas Eve festivities today. Mom made ham and her cheesy casserole, the same one I didn't eat at Easter. This time, I had a normal meal, one that was actually physically and emotionally satisfying, and yes, it included a few spoonfuls of the casserole, which I savored and thoroughly enjoyed... and then I got on with my night. Fuck, later, while we watched The Santa Clause with Olivia, I had a few Christmas cookies and cocoa, too.

No guilt, no shame, no feeling like I needed to hurry to the track to "work it off."

What a difference a year can make, huh? When Nate made his typical fat jokes, I ignored him completely. He hates being ignored, which made him try harder, but I continued to ignore him. Eventually, he stopped. A Christmas miracle!

Mia and I gave my mom a lovely turquoise necklace because it's my mom's favorite. Mia found the necklace, brought it home, and told me that if I hated it, we could exchange it, but it was perfect.

We gave Olivia a microscope, because she's been saying she wants to be a doctor. Mia's background in medical research and her biology degree meant she was the perfect person to teach Olivia how to use it. They spent a good hour on that, and I stayed back. It warmed my heart to watch them bond that way, to know Mia was trying to make sure Olivia felt important to her, too... and it made me realize what an amazing mom Mia's going to be when the time comes. She's so patient. She makes Olivia laugh... She can be really shy around new people, but Mia drew her out. I think that's going to help a lot when

I leave next weekend.

I keep feeling like I should pinch myself because this feels like a dream. A wonderful, cozy, beautiful Christmas dream. It feels too good to be true, but I'm letting myself believe in it. I've cast away my doubts, as much as someone with anxiety ever can, and I am giving everything that I am and everything that I have to make this work with Mia.

Vanessa stopped by for a quick visit after dinner with her family, since Garwood's only the next town over and less than ten minutes away. She seems happier than she's ever been, even though it's only been a month since her breakup with Pete. She found a cute little studio apartment down the shore. I know she loves being close to the water.

Mia and I gave her the present we'd picked out for her. We found it in a little gallery near Mia's apartment just last week, and I immediately knew it was the perfect Christmas/apartment-warming combo gift. It's a stunning watercolor of a mermaid sunbathing on a rock with a dreamy expression on her face. Van and I used to pretend to be mermaids in my grandparents' pool, and we both have a soft spot for them as a result, so I told Mia, and she said it had to be that.

I was so excited to give it to her that you'd think I was the one getting the gift.

"Oh my god... Mia, Tess. I love it so much. It's perfect!" she cried. "I'm going to hang it over my bed when I get home tonight."

She left not long after, and Mia said to me, "what do you think about introducing her to Ryan?"

I laughed because I honestly had been thinking the same thing just last weekend when he was at our party. I don't know why, but I can totally see those two hitting it off. I know she's not ready yet, but it's so funny that Mia - who knows Ryan so well - and I - who know Van so well - had the same instinct about those two. So, we'll see.

Around 7:00, we got a rare treat, and it started to snow. I love snow on Christmas Eve, and I always feel like it just doesn't happen as often as you'd think in the Northeast. Mia said that when she was growing up in Colorado, they had snow most years, which I think sounds lovely. I've always wanted to go there, and she promised to take me with her whenever she has to go to deal with her mother's estate.

While I am sad that she'll have to do that, I am glad that she's going to get to show me where she grew up, a place that I know she loves deeply. Not that she doesn't love NYC, but she has a tattoo of a snowy mountain scene on her left hip, and it has the word "home" in script below it. She said the mountains are where she feels most "her," which is funny because I've always been obsessed with mountains. One of my big dreams has been to see a snow-capped mountain. She said we can make that happen. I warned her that there's a good chance I'm going to get emotional when I do and might even cry. She told me she can handle it.

I don't doubt her for a minute.

We drove with Olivia to the center of town, near the train station, where they have a cute sleigh with light-up reindeer. Mia took a picture of me and Livvy together.

Then Olivia asked me if I'd take one of her and Mia, and that melted my heart, but not nearly as much as when, a few minutes later, Mia gave Olivia another gift, one I didn't know about.

It was a small box, and when she unwrapped it, I saw Tiffany blue. Olivia also loves that movie, so she lit up brighter than the lights behind her when she opened it. It was a necklace with an engraved heart. On the back, it said, "you're always in our hearts."

Olivia squealed, "oh, Mia... I love it. Can you help me?"

Mia put it on her and said, "Olivia, I know how much you love your sister. I want you to know that while I don't think I could ever love her as much as you do, I am going

166

to try with all my heart, and I promise you I will take very good care of her for you, okay?"

"I'm really gonna miss her," Olivia said, biting her lip and trying not to cry.

"I know you are, sweetie, but I want you to know that she - WE - will be there for you whenever you need to talk to us, okay? You can visit us, and we'll come here to visit you, too."

"Promise?" Livvy asked, her blue eyes wide, her auburn hair shimmering as it blew around her in the wind.

"I promise," Mia told her.

"Okay. Just please make sure you do take care of her, okay? 'Cause I really need her."

"I know you do, and you know what? I need her, too." Mia reached out her hand to me, and I joined them for a group hug.

Then we headed back to the house, read *Twas The Night Before Christmas* out loud, taking turns, and we tucked Olivia into bed.

"Remember, I'll be back tomorrow afternoon, okay?" I told her. "You can show me what Santa brought you."

"Okay. I love you, Tessa."

"I love you too, Livvy. So, so much."

After that, we said goodnight to my mom, and Mia and I headed home together, back to her... our apartment. We stopped by Rockefeller Center on the way home, just to see the tree briefly. Mia promised to bring me back to skate next week. I laughed because I'm pretty sure that's going to be a trainwreck. I haven't been skating since I was 16, but I have always loved it, and skating at Rockefeller Center is another one of my lifelong dreams, which I pointed out.

"I know," Mia said, with a sexy little smile, "and it's my goal in life to make as many of those dreams reality as I possibly can."

Then I kissed her by the ginormous tree... we held hands while walking back to the waiting cab. We made out like teenagers in the backseat, with Mia practically sitting on my lap. Thankfully, most NYC cab drivers are immune to this sort of thing. I'm sure they've seen worse!

Now we're ensconced in Mia's apartment with her little wood-burning fireplace roaring (finding one of those in NYC is like hitting the lottery, or so I'm told, but I love it). I'm snuggled up against her chest, her arms wrapped around me, as I write this, and I know she's reading over my shoulder.

Which leads me to ask, *Mia... will you marry me?*

She's grabbing the pen... and giggling. Seems like a good sign for me.

Yes, Tessa... I will marry you. In fact, I have your ring in my dresser drawer and was going to ask you to be my wife tomorrow morning. I should've known you'd beat me to it!

XOXO,
Mia

And that, Dear Book, seems like the perfect place to say...

goodbye, With Love,
Tessa Elizabeth Alexander

Acknowledgments

This book would not exist without National Novel Writing Month (NaNoWriMo). If you are not familiar with this annual event, the goal is to write a novel (at least 50,000 words) during the month of November. There's a great community, if that is your thing, but you can also go it alone. I'd thought about doing NaNoWriMo for several years, but the death of my beloved high school English teacher (to whom this book is dedicated) prompted me to finally do it.

Jean scared a lot of the students, and she was definitely tough, but she was exactly who I needed in a writing teacher at that point in my life. Jean also let me publish a semi-steamy short story in our lit mag one year, so I like to think that all the sex in this book would not even remotely phase her. It saddens me that she will not get to tell me what I could've done better while also praising what I did well.

To Barbara, who was part guidance counselor, part teacher, part surrogate mother, and part therapist, I would not be who I am today without having had you in my life. Thank you for everything you have done for me over the years.

To Sue, you saw a neglected toddler in a pink snowsuit, and you never stopped wondering if she was okay. When you found her again, you made sure she knew how much she meant to you. I love you. You are my chosen family.

To Heather, thank you for being my personal cheerleader. I love you and am grateful for your friendship all these years. You inspired Tessa's name with your sweet gift. I have no idea what she might've been called if not for you. Quack!

To my other wonderful friends, I love you, and I am lucky to have you in my life.

To Monika, you took a vague idea and a color palette, and you created the cover of my dreams. You gave Tessa life with your art. Thank you!

To the person who gave me a diary for Christmas in 1998, thank you. I hadn't kept one in years, but I did so faithfully until the following Christmas, just like Tessa. Unlike Tessa, I went through about six blank books in the process. Also unlike Tessa, mine have long since been destroyed.

To the fat activists who inspire me daily, among them Marilyn Wann (author of *Fat!So?*), Lindley Ashline, and Ragen Chastain, thank you for what you do. I wish I had found the movement in 1999, but I am glad I found it when I did.

To my beloved little dog Yogi, I love you. Thank you for making me laugh, even on my worst days. No, he can't read, but if any dog could, it would be him.

To Phoenix, thank you for helping me figure shit out over the past couple of years. Thank you for not being irritatingly prompt. Thank you for hating diet culture bullshit right along with me. You are just what I needed in a therapist.

To my readers, I hope you enjoyed Tessa's journey.

Thank you for being here and for helping me make my childhood dream come true!

Finally, to my husband Thomas, the other person to whom this book is dedicated, who is my editor, publisher, comma savior, marketing director, the order in my chaos, and the most remarkable person I've ever known... thank you is insufficient. As I thought on July 4th, 1999, I never fell out of love with you, and I know I never will.

I've always read author acknowledgments at the ends of books, and I have long imagined what I might write in my own, so I can't lie - this was a thrill. Thank you for being a part of it!

XOXO,
Juliet

Thanks for reading!

Visit iamjulietjames.com or scan the QR code below to join Juliet's mailing list and to be informed of upcoming news, events, and releases.

XOXO,
Juliet

www.ingramcontent.com/pod-product-compliance
Lightning Source LLC
Chambersburg PA
CBHW032011170626
46807CB00006B/2752

9798988890423